Lottie's Journey

Leah Brewer

Copyright © 2025 Leah Brewer

The characters and events portrayed in this book are fictitious. Any similarity to real persons, living or dead, is coincidental and not intended by the author.

All rights reserved. No part of this book may be reproduced, stored in a retrieval system, or transmitted in any form or by any means, electronic, mechanical, photocopying, recording, or otherwise, without the express permission of the author.

ISBN-13: 979-8-9864921-7-9

Cover design by Leah Brewer; Front Cover Image photo by Shelby Biggers from SMB Photography.

Scripture is taken from the New King James Version®. Copyright © 1982 by Thomas Nelson. Used by permission. All rights reserved.

This book is dedicated to my late Aunt Lottie and my granddaughter Charlotte, affectionately known as our little Lottie (Lot Lot).

Author's Note

Before you begin reading this book, please be aware that it addresses themes of drug use, addiction, and the challenges of physical and mental abuse. While the book avoids explicit language and steamy romance, it features a closed-door romance filled with suspense and danger.

In addition to new characters, some of your favorite characters from the first three Seeds of Faith books will also appear in Lottie's Journey.

My aim for this novel is to provide support to those who may be grappling with addiction and/or abuse.

I pray you have a blessed day,
Leah

Chapter 1

MIAMI

The tiny camper trailer seemed to breathe every time the wind blew. Raised voices seeped from beneath the rickety bathroom door. This was the first time Lottie McKenna had been inside the place Eddie Chambers, her ex-boyfriend, called home.

From the look of things, it could be her last.

She pressed her fingers to her forehead and closed her hazel eyes. When she opened them, her gaze landed on a streak of blue toothpaste smeared inside the dull green sink. A bottle of Always Save mint mouthwash, Colgate toothpaste, a razor, and black hairs filled the space around the sink.

She peered inside the tiny shower stall and grimaced at the streaks of funk. The shower had seen better days. Would it kill him to throw some cleaning bubbles in there on occasion?

What was wrong with her? She should be thinking of a way to get out of there without another fight, not judging Eddie's housekeeping skills.

Over the years, she'd become skilled at pretending things were okay. But today wasn't the day to do that.

The scent of a recently killed skunk on the side of the road drifted into the bathroom, stinging her nostrils. Great. Now the threesome was in there getting high.

Sobs wrenched her insides as she stared at her beaten and bloody face in the dirty bathroom mirror. As she dabbed blood from her nose with wadded-up toilet paper, a strand of artic blonde hair fell out of her bun, tumbling across her forehead. She tucked it behind her ear before lowering herself onto the tiny plastic toilet.

Every lousy decision she'd made in her forty-one years had brought her to this point.

She needed to think. When Eddie called last week, he promised he'd changed. He said he needed to make things right with her and their sixteen-year-old, Rhnae. Why had she listened to him? How could she be so stupid?

She ran a jerky hand through her hair. She knew exactly why she listened. The slight chance he would be the man she and Rhnae needed caused her to shut the voice of reason down.

A pang hit Lottie's stomach as regret washed over her for all the heartache she'd caused Rhnae. She'd give anything to go back and raise her baby girl differently. She'd hoped Eddie felt the same way. All she'd wanted was to see if he was off drugs like he'd promised. She had to make sure, before she allowed him back into their daughter's life.

Instead, she'd put herself in a volatile situation. Eddie had attacked her when she spurned his advances, and with the way her body felt, she figured he'd slipped something in her coffee. There's no telling what he would've done if visitors hadn't stopped by. That's when she escaped to the bathroom.

A weird feeling settled in her belly, causing her to pause. She closed her eyes. Why had she accepted that cup of coffee? Because she was the same scared little girl she'd always been when it came to Eddie Chambers.

A raised voice came from the other end of the camper trailer. "You still going with us, man? Or has your old lady changed your mind?" Lottie recognized the voice. Ozzie Hicks, a man known for his illegal ways.

"Funny. Lottie ain't my old lady," a nervous chuckle came from Eddie. "She just stopped by to guilt trip me over our daughter."

"You sure she ain't no nark?"

"Lottie? Working with the cops? No way, man."

"Why don't you and Buck leave me alone with her so I can find out for myself." Ozzie's voice dripped with meanness.

Lottie clutched her stomach. Her heart rate accelerated, pounding into her throat like a bumper car with a deranged driver behind the wheel. She eased out of the bathroom. Maybe she could sneak out.

"There ain't no way I'd ever leave you alone with Lottie." Eddie's tone caused Lottie's heart to stir. If she didn't know better, she'd think he still cared about her. Not likely since he'd stayed out of her life for over ten years and then attacked her within minutes of seeing her today.

"Then what are we waiting for? Let's go get what's ours," Buck Hicks, Ozzie's slimy cousin, said. "That broad ain't worth fighting over."

Lottie charged a few paces down the hall. Her legs tingled with every step. Eddie and Buck sat on the tan built-in sofa while Ozzie lounged at the small dining table.

One look at Eddie, with his thinning brown hair limp on his shoulders, made Lottie want to throttle him. He had aged well beyond his forty-three years.

When they'd first met, he had a head full of dark brown hair and reminded her of an actor on a show she couldn't quite place at the moment. His family owned several grocery stores, and he had plenty of money back then. She'd heard that he lost everything a year or so after his parents died. Drugs had taken everything from him. His looks. His wealth. His family.

Hoots of laughter echoed from Ozzie. "What happened to your face?" He slapped Eddie's knee. "No wonder you ain't wanting to go nowhere."

Even though her throat stung, she still managed to raise her voice. She glared at Ozzie and then

Buck, her gaze landing on his bald head before meeting his eyes. "What are you talking about?"

Buck opened his mouth, but Ozzie raised a hand, stopping him from speaking. Ozzie's thick lips set into a flat line as he stared at Lottie. "You need to mind your own business before you get taught another lesson."

She turned to Eddie, her voice raising a few more octaves. Pain coursed through every bone and muscle in her face. "Don't you care anything about Rhnae?"

Eddie's shoulder raised and froze in place. "I got things going on, Lot. You should have at least called before showing up on my doorstep." His eyes held a smidge of regret. "You caught me at a bad time."

What nerve he had. He was the one who asked her to come.

Instead of erupting, she consciously lowered her voice. As she spoke, another strange sensation washed over her. "Rhnae will be a senior in high school soon. You need to make things right with her," she insisted, her voice weak. He might let her go without another beating if she made him think she still wanted him to get to know Rhnae.

A shallow dip of a frown etched across his face. "What do you think I'm trying to do?"

Lottie pushed back the nausea as bitter laughter flowed. "Seems to me you're still working on destroying your life. Look at who you're spending your time with. A couple of thugs more interested in their next high than anything else."

Ozzie bolted out of his seat. He pinned Lottie against the mini refrigerator. Pain sliced through her spine and elbow. "You keep your mouth shut," he said.

The top of the refrigerator cut into her back. "Let go of me." Lottie attempted to sound tough. Instead, her words came out slurred. She blinked and licked her lips. There was no doubt she'd been drugged.

Eddie shoved Ozzie away from Lottie so hard he fell into the door, tumbling outside. Eddie jumped through the open space and landed on Ozzie, punching his face.

Lottie stumbled outside with Buck right behind her. The last of the sun dipped behind the trees, leaving behind a dark and mottled sky, which seemed fitting for the situation. Even though the sun had all but disappeared, the muggy July heat came close to suffocating Lottie. Even the high wind carried a burning sensation every time it hit her face.

Buck grabbed her by the throat and shoved a gun into her side. "Get up, or she's dead."

Her head swam, and she felt herself clinging to Buck. If not, she'd hit the ground. Dread pooled in her stomach. That and more waves of nausea.

An older woman poked her head out of the camper next door. "You hooligans need to stop that," she said before disappearing inside.

Eddie hauled himself up. Ozzie slammed his fist into Eddie's face. Out of nowhere, a knife appeared in Eddie's hand.

The sound of a gunshot echoed across the yard. Eddie fell to the ground and stayed still. Buck and Ozzie jumped into a rusty white Dodge minivan and sped away.

Lottie's knees buckled.

A few minutes later, sirens sounded in the distance. Her eyes squeezed shut. Footsteps crunched on the gravel driveway, and someone yelled for her to get up. She tried, but her body wouldn't cooperate.

What was she doing here? Was she still in Florida? Where was she?

The yelling intensified. She blinked a few times, doing her best to focus on the person lying on the ground. Who could that be? Her legs were as heavy as an antique couch as she attempted to crawl to the person. She needed to know who it was. Shouldn't she try to help?

Someone grabbed her shoulder. She jerked away and slung her fist. She nearly rejoiced when her knuckles cracked into their jaw. That'll teach them to try to accost Lottie McKenna.

Her celebration came to a swift end as spasms racked the muscles in her chest. Clicking, accompanied by deep and fiery slices of pain, overtook her body. A dark figure holding a tazer towered over her.

They pinned her to the ground. She sucked in a labored breath that didn't reach her lungs. The weight on her chest seemed determined to suffocate her to death. Before she could say she couldn't breathe, her eyes grew heavy. The last thing she heard was someone shouting that she was under arrest.

Chapter 2

Silence fell over the courtroom while Lottie waited for the judge to hand down her sentence. Even the room full of onlookers seemed anxious to see how things would end for her.

Simon Wheeler, her attorney and dear friend from Arkansas, offered her a comforting smile. She glanced at the turquoise ring shaped like a bird on his right middle finger. Whenever her nerves became unsettled, she focused on that ring, which somehow helped calm her mind.

Lottie still found it hard to believe that Simon and his wife, Vandon, traveled all the way to Miami to assist her. Fortunately for Lottie, Simon was licensed to practice in both Florida and Arkansas, thanks to a high-profile client with connections in multiple states.

Judge Mooneyhan looked over his black-rimmed glasses. "Miss McKenna, I understand your desire to bring your family back together. Unfortunately, things didn't turn out the way you hoped. I'm sorry for your loss, but I hope you can move forward. Due to the circumstances of your situation and how you were drugged without your knowledge, all charges are dropped. You're free to go."

Vandon clapped her hands together.

Simon glanced at Vandon before turning to the Judge. "Thank you, your honor."

Lottie folded her hands under her chin and mouthed thank you.

Eddie's sister, Shannon Gomez, glared at Lottie on the way out of the courthouse. "You just couldn't leave my brother alone, could you? Now he's dead because of you."

Lottie swallowed the sob. "I'm sorry for your loss, Shannon. Truly, but his death is not my fault. He called me, not the other way around."

Shannon leaned close enough to Lottie that she could tell she had recently drunk a cup of strong coffee that verged on being burned. "Not your fault, my foot. Now that he's dead and buried, what are you going to do about Rhnae?"

"Same as always. Take care of her by myself." Lottie took one last look at Shannon and shook her head as Vandon led Lottie down the steps.

Shannon kept mouthing as they drove away in Simon's black rental Tahoe. A few minutes later, Simon zipped around a tow truck in a hotel parking lot. "Lottie, we reserved a room for you for tonight. I figured we'd head to Pensacola in the morning."

"That sounds perfect," Lottie said. "Thank you both for returning my rental car to Enterprise and everything else. I don't know what I would've done without you." She bit her bottom lip.

"We love you to pieces, Lottie." Vandon cocked her head. "Don't ever forget it."

The following day, Vandon swiveled around and handed Lottie a pillow and fuzzy blanket. "I figured you'd need to rest on the drive to Pensacola."

"You're so thoughtful," Lottie said as she accepted the items.

What seemed like a few minutes later, Lottie jerked awake. She dragged in a breath, half expecting to see Eddie standing beside her with a knife.

After blinking a few times, she remembered she was on her way home. She'd stop by her niece, Frankie's to pick Rhnae up before heading to their cabin. Lottie lived and worked at Frankie's campground that had several cabins they rented out and they even held a Christmas festival to benefit the Children's Home.

Soft snores mixed with a jazz tune drifted from the front seat. Simon lowered the volume and glanced at Lottie. "Both you and my Vandon have been sound asleep. How are you feeling?"

"Honestly, I'm a bit out of sorts," Lottie said as she glanced out the window at the Destin sign. "I can't believe I slept so long."

"You needed it."

Lottie nodded, grabbed a water bottle from the ice chest, and chugged it. She rubbed her neck before closing her eyes and drifting back off.

Around three o'clock, they pulled into the driveway of Alex and Frankie's home. Lottie hopped out and let herself in through the back door.

Raised voices echoed down the hallway. "You're more of a mother to me than Lottie McKenna has ever been or ever will be," Rhnae said.

Lottie pressed her hand firmly over her mouth, trying to hold back the wave of emotion threatening to spill over. Tears welled in her eyes as she took a shaky breath.

"You don't really mean that," Frankie said softly, concern in her voice.

"Yes, I do," Rhnae replied, her voice trembling with intensity. "You have no idea what my life has been like. The way that woman treated me was nothing short of torment."

"But you forgave her," Frankie reminded Rhnae gently.

"Yeah, I did," Rhnae admitted, her gaze drifting to the floor. "But I really thought she'd changed this time. I wanted to believe she was different."

"She has changed," Frankie insisted, her tone earnest. "You just need to give it time."

"Then why did she go see Eddie? Her actions got him killed." Rhnae sobbed, and Lottie strained to hear what she said next. "Lottie is the same lying piece of garbage she's always been."

The air in Lottie's lungs evaporated.

Frankie gasped. "You don't mean that."

"Yes, I do. I'm better off without her. If you'd been there for the mental and physical abuse I've dealt with my whole life, you'd agree."

"Oh, Rhnae. I'm so sorry."

"I'm going to my room. Please tell that woman to leave me alone. I don't want or need her in my life."

A tight fist constricted around Lottie's heart as she peeked around the corner of the door. Rhnae stormed down the hallway in the other direction.

Frankie turned and met Lottie's gaze. Her hand raised, beckoning Lottie to come close, but Lottie's legs refused to move inside. Instead, she turned and bolted back the way she'd come. She had to get as far away from that house as possible.

Chapter 3

THEN: 2013

The scent of rotten garbage wafted through the air. Lottie's eyes opened to a slit. Somehow, she'd fallen off the mattress onto the floor. She tried to sit up, but her head pounded.

After taking a few breaths, she pulled the curtain back an inch and peered out the window. A gray Ford Focus sat in their neighbor's yard. She squinted her eyes. That same car had been following her around. What could they want from her? Her heart raced as she stared out the window.

"Mommy?" Rhnae, Lottie's five-year-old daughter, stared at her with wide, round eyes. She clutched an empty cereal bag to her chest, clinging to it like a lifeline.

"Oh, hey, Rhnae," Lottie said as she crawled over a pile of dirty clothes into the bathroom. She touched her face and gagged. Dried vomit clung to her cheeks and matted her hair.

As she turned the water faucet on, she tried remembering what she'd done the night before, but her mind was blank. The pipes groaned, but no water came out. That's right, the city had turned her water off. Another bill she'd forgotten to pay.

Rhnae tugged on Lottie's t-shirt. "I'm hungry."

Lottie grabbed a washrag off the floor and stumbled toward the kitchen. She picked up a half-full bottle of whiskey that lay against the wall. This was just what she needed to help ease her headache. She took a swig from the bottle.

"Mommy, do we have anything to eat?" Rhnae asked, her voice low as her stomach grumbled softly.

Lottie sighed, her patience wearing thin. "Quit being so selfish," she snapped, pressing her fingers against her temples in an effort to ease the throbbing pain in her head. "My head is killing me, and all you can think about is how hungry you are!"

With her lower lip quivering, Rhnae looked at Lottie with wide, pleading eyes. "I'm sorry," she murmured.

As Lottie caught sight of Rhnae's greasy hair and the smudges of dirt on her cheeks, a wave of sympathy washed over her. "Come on, let's see what we can find in the kitchen," Lottie said, her tone softening as she reached out, gently squeezing Rhnae's shoulder.

Instantly, Rhnae's expression transformed. Her eyes sparkled with hope, and a smile spread across her face. "Okay, Mommy! Thank you!" she exclaimed, her excitement evident as she followed Lottie into the kitchen to find something to eat.

Rhnae crawled onto a wooden chair and leaned her elbows onto the matching table as Lottie opened the cabinet. When Lottie found that table and chair set at Goodwill, she'd begged Eddie to buy it. It was exactly like her mom's table in their eat-in kitchen when Lottie was a kid.

Empty cupboards stared back at her. Where was all the food she'd bought? They should have at least a few packs of ramen noodles and chips. She scratched her head. How long had she been out?

Luckily, the next cabinet held some pancake mix and oil. But she needed water to make pancakes. "Run out to my car and see if you can find any water bottles."

"Okay," Rhnae said as she skipped out the front door. Within a few minutes, she came back with four water bottles.

Lottie grabbed one and poured some of it on the washrag. She scrubbed the dried vomit off her face and used the rest in the pancake mix.

As the pancake sizzled in the pan, she rummaged through her purse for her hydrocodone. She popped one in her mouth and washed it down with the last of the whiskey.

Feeling a sense of relief that the throbbing headache would soon subside, Lottie flipped the pancake in the skillet, watching it sizzle as it cooked. The aroma of warm batter filled the kitchen, momentarily distracting her from the dull ache in her temples. Turning her attention to Rhnae, she asked, "What happened to the food I bought?"

With a small, sheepish smile, Rhnae replied, "I ate it, Mommy. I'm really sorry." Her voice carried a hint of guilt, as she glanced down, avoiding Lottie's gaze.

Lottie raised an eyebrow, trying to process what she had just heard. "You ate it all last night?"

Rhnae held up two fingers, a glint of tears in her eyes. "The last two nights."

Lottie nodded. She must have been out longer than she'd realized, then. The nights blurred together in her memory. At least Rhnae was responsible enough to take care of herself. "Have you seen your daddy?"

"He left when you went to sleep," Rhnae answered, her eyes on the skillet.

That figured. No telling which woman he'd been with this time. Lottie was getting tired of being a doormat. She needed to find a way out. Her eyes lingered on her purse, and she reached for the bottle of Xanax Eddie brought her after his last drug-induced rampage. Thankfully, Rhnae had been with Eddie's sister Shannon at the time, so she didn't have to witness Lottie's beat down.

After making a second pancake, Lottie set the plate on the glass dining table. "You'll have to use some grape jelly on the pancakes. We don't have any syrup."

"Oh, I just love grape jelly, Mommy."

After Lottie spread the jelly on top, Rhnae shoveled a huge bite in her mouth. "Mmm. Don't you want some?"

Waves of nausea threatened to overtake Lottie. She gripped the metal chair until it passed. "Yeah, I need to eat."

Twenty minutes later, Lottie stumbled back into her bedroom and fell onto the mattress. She shoved her hand underneath it and pulled out another bottle of whiskey and an empty plastic baggie. Her heart dropped as she jerked the side table drawer open. The drawer fell out and landed on the floor with a thud. Her eyes widened as she grabbed a pocketknife. She turned the baggie inside out and scraped it, searching for even a small trace of leftover meth. She stuck it inside a dirty cup and poured whiskey over it. After getting all she could, she sucked on the corner of the baggie, hoping Eddie would be home soon with a refill.

Rhnae walked inside the room and stopped at the foot of the bed.

Lottie wadded the baggie up, shoved it between the mattress and springs, and patted the space beside her. Rhnae grinned before crawling onto the bed.

Even though Lottie knew she should stay sober, she twisted the lid off the whiskey bottle and took a swig. At least until today, she hadn't taken Xanax for a while. That was a good thing. Right?

She kissed Rhnae's forehead before turning her attention to the TV. A Disney princess sang something about letting go. If only life were that easy. She'd give anything to let go.

Chapter 4

No matter what Lottie did, she'd never be good enough for Rhnae. She shoved past a bewildered-looking Simon and Vandon and climbed into the 2018 white Jeep Cherokee she'd bought two months earlier. Tears threatened to blind her as she backed the Jeep out onto the road. She opened it up when she reached the interstate heading toward Destin.

It had been almost a year since she'd felt like she was on a downward spiral. At this moment, she had to be in a dream world. The one where the devil wins. So maybe she was in a horrific nightmare where she'd wake up soon.

What made her go see Eddie? Had she really thought something good would come from it? Or was Rhnae right? Had Lottie been after the thrill of the high Eddie seemed to always give her?

If only she could go back and never pop that first pill. If only she could go back and never take that first drink of alcohol. If only she could go back and never decide taking meth was a good idea.

She'd even settle for returning to the moment she thought getting Rhnae and her dad back together was a good idea and changing her mind. But she couldn't.

After driving a while, she pulled over at a pharmacy in Mary Esther. Her hands shook uncontrollably as she took several deep breaths. A thought passed through her mind as she stared out the windshield. A few drinks of whiskey could help calm her nerves.

After searching Google Maps, she eased onto the road, heading straight toward the one thing she knew would help her forget her troubles—a liquor store.

Within a few minutes, she held the brown-bagged bottle in her lap. It burned her legs so badly that she moved it to the passenger seat. That didn't make sense. It held no heat. It had to be Lottie's imagination. It surely wasn't guilt that caused it.

No one wanted her around, so what did she have to feel guilty about? Rhnae was right. Frankie would make a much better mother than she ever had. She picked up the bag and then set it down. It would be best if she found somewhere to stop. The beach sounded like a perfect place to calm her nerves.

Satisfied with her plan, she pressed the gas pedal and headed toward Fort Walton Beach. She pulled into the welcome center and slipped out of her Jeep.

She kept a fold-up chair in her trunk since she lived so close to the ocean. She grabbed it and bee-lined to the water. A seagull greeted her as it flew by. Usually, she would smile. Not today. Maybe never again.

Her feet sunk into the soft white sand, but she trudged through until she reached the water's edge. A few people frolicked in the waves, and even fewer lounged on the shore. Lottie ignored them and pulled her brown-bagged friend out of her tote bag.

A young girl who looked to be around ten squealed. Lottie cut her eyes in that direction. The girl and a woman, probably her mother, had tumbled in the waves close to the shore. They both laughed as they held onto one another.

Lottie looked away as jealousy and longing filled her bones. She'd give anything to live an everyday life. Her face hardened with a mask of anger. That life wasn't in the cards for her.

Stinging tears filled her eyes, and a cry rose within. She was no good to anyone. Rhnae would be better off if Lottie disappeared. Frankie and Alex would give Rhnae a good home and future. Much better than Lottie would ever be able to.

A scream sliced through the air. "My son!"

Lottie's eyes panned the beach. A toddler's head bobbed out of the waves directly in front of her. She sprang to her feet and torpedoed into the wa-ter toward a blue and white cap. The toddler went under just as Lottie laid her hands on him. She raced toward the shore and handed him to the same woman who'd been playing in the water with the little girl. The toddler coughed and spit before letting out a loud cry, telling Lottie his lungs were fine. The woman sobbed what sounded like a thank you.

Within minutes, paramedics determined the little boy, Brayden, would be okay. His daddy, watching him while the mom played in the waves with his sister, had dozed off because his blood sugar dropped too low.

"Ma'am?" The woman grasped Lottie's hands. "Thank you for saving our little boy."

Lottie swallowed and lowered her eyes. "I'm glad I was there."

"If you hadn't been, I'm sure things wouldn't have turned out this well." She let go of Lottie's hands. "I'm Samantha Silverton."

Samantha's gaze lingered on Lottie's lightly bruised face, but thankfully, she didn't comment. "Lottie McKenna. Glad to make your acquaintance."

Samantha pressed a business card into Lottie's hand. "If you ever need anything, please don't hesitate to reach out. I only live a few minutes away.

"I appreciate that," Lottie said as she stuffed the card in her pocket.

After the family left, Lottie stared at the waves beating onto the shore for a few minutes, recounting all that had happened. She still couldn't believe it. How crazy was it that she chose this beach at this exact time?

She pulled the woman's business card out of her pocket. Her eyes misted when she read it.

Chapter 5

The business card in Lottie's hand seemed to burn the spot she pressed it on her chest. Tears trickled down her cheeks as she played the events that led to Eddie's death through her mind for the hundredth time. She still couldn't believe he fought Ozzie over her. Especially after working her over the way he had.

The unopened bottle of whiskey taunted her. Sweet water tickled her throat as she contemplated taking a sip. Just one to ease her mind. Her phone buzzed. Frankie. She stared at the phone until it was silent. A minute later, a voicemail alert popped across the screen.

Lottie's hand hovered over the button. What did she have to lose? She hit play and held her breath. Frankie's sweet voice mixed with the waves and seagulls. *"Aunt Lottie, please call me back. I'm sorry for what Rhnae said. You know she's hurting right now. She needs you. We all do. I love you."*

Lottie closed her eyes as she played the message a second time. It didn't seem possible that Lottie and Frankie had only met the year before. Helen, Frankie's mother, and Lottie's sister had passed away years earlier, and then Larry, Helen's husband, a few years later.

Lottie and Helen had been orphans. Helen had been the good sister while Lottie checked every box to wear the title of rebellious teenager. Lottie ran away from the children's home and they never reconnected before Helen passed.

Another regret Lottie lived with.

There was no sense in letting Frankie worry. Not to mention Simon and Vandon. Lottie sighed and picked up the phone, dialing Frankie's number.

"Aunt Lottie?"

"Listen, Frankie, I'm fine." She picked up the business card and made a decision. "I've decided to check into a rehab."

"You have?"

"I think that's best. Right now, I'm struggling. Do you mind if I take off work for a while?"

"Of course not. Take all the time you need. You know Alex and I will support you however we can."

"I appreciate that. Will you tell Rhnae I love her?"

"I sure will."

"Oh, and take care of Dreamy?"

Frankie giggled. "I think Dreamy gets fed better than our customers. Alex loves that cat."

Dreamy, the cat, had adopted Lottie and Frankie the year before, when he showed up at the cabins Frankie had inherited from her late father. Lottie named him Dreamy because he reminded her of a Dreamsicle ice cream bar with his orange and white coloring.

"You're probably right. Thank you for everything. I love you."

"Please keep us posted. I love you, too."

Once Lottie hung up, she glanced at the sky. Pink blended into a bright orange, reminding her of the last time she'd been on the beach at sunset. Rhnae had wanted to take some family pictures, so they had dressed up and decided to take them at about this time.

She stood and grabbed her bag. After slipping into the Welcome Center's bathroom, she un-screwed the top of the bottle and, with trembling hands, poured it down the sink. She pitched the empty container in the trash can and walked out with a newfound determination. She would be the mother Rhnae needed, no matter what.

After entering the address on the back of the business card into her navigation, she gradually merged into traffic. The rehab facility was about an hour away. Minutes into her drive, the sky shifted to dark shades of black and blue, with a few pale streaks. Figuring it was too late to check into the rehab, she pulled into the parking lot of what looked to be a pay-by-the-hour motel. Hotels in this area were way too expensive, so this one would have to do. The tan building had two rows of rooms with an office in the front. It reminded Lottie of a place where a killer would go to plot his next move. She clicked her tongue at her foolishness and claimed a parking spot toward the back of the building.

A toned man wearing loose black shorts, a gray t-shirt, and a black ballcap leaned against the trunk of a Camaro so black it seemed almost purple. He cut his eyes in her direction and sighed. She couldn't believe it. The man looked annoyed that she parked within his vicinity.

"Lady, I need you to get back in your car and go somewhere else." His voice came out husky, almost smoky.

Lottie put her hand on her hip. "Am I bothering you?"

"Yes. Go. Now." The smokiness changed to a tune Lottie would call nothing but whiney as he pointed at her Jeep. Headlights shined in her eyes as a black SUV crept into the parking lot. It pulled into a spot across from where they stood. "Lady, I asked you to leave. Please go now."

Two men emerged from the imposing silhouette of a Ford Expedition, their presence sending a chill down Lottie's spine. The taller of the two had an air of menace about him, while the other, wiry and with jet-black slicked-back hair, twirled a switchblade between his fingers, the blade gleaming ominously in the dim light.

Tension crackled in the air, and there was no doubt in her mind that they were up to no good. Just behind her, the man groaned and released a deep, shaky breath, clearly uneasy about the unfolding situation.

"What's your name, lady?" he inquired, his voice low and threatening.

"Lottie. Why do you want to know?" she replied, trying to hide the tremor in her voice.

"I'm Barrett," he said, his gaze fixed on the thugs as he positioned himself protectively in front of her. "And I hope you're a good actress."

"Why would I need to act?" she shot back, her forehead creasing.

"Because," Barrett replied, his tone urgent, "both of our lives may depend on it. Please, just play along."

The wiry man sauntered closer, his eyes narrowing as he assessed Lottie with a predatory glint. "Who do we have here?"

Barrett moved to the left, almost shielding Lottie from view. "The lady is with me."

She could barely see over his shoulder. Her chin brushed against the fabric of his T-shirt as she peeked around him. The scent of Snuggle fabric softener snagged her senses.

The wiry man tilted his head, narrowing his eyes further. "Why is she here?" he questioned, his grip tightening on the switchblade as he studied the scene before him.

"I asked her to meet me here at eight." Barrett shrugged. "She's early."

The wiry man tapped his chin with the knife's edge as his gaze perused Lottie. "Where do I know you from?"

Her neck went taut as she met his gaze. "I don't know."

Recognition lit his dark eyes, and he bounced on his toes. "I know who you are. We was in the same orphanage before we ran away together. Lottie McKenna!"

Oh no. Her heart plummeted as she came face to face with a blast from her past. "Coco?"

Surely, her luck wasn't so bad that she'd meet up with Coco Flores. Not after all those years. He seemed more dangerous now than ever. He and his companion looked like they stepped out of a scene of Fast and Furious. Her eyes lingered on a gun sticking out of the muscular man's jeans.

"I knew it was you." He said as he picked her up and quickly kissed her lips. "You lost weight."

Her spine stiffened as she backed away from Coco. What mess had she stumbled into? She wasn't sure but she had a feeling she'd walked out of the fire in Miami only to land in the flames in Destin.

Chapter 6

William Barrett Donahue considered, and not for the first time this night, that he might be in over his head. He squared his posture and met Coco's gaze head-on.

Even though he had concerns that the woman knew Coco, he followed his instincts. Her shoulders trembled next to his. It didn't matter how they knew one another. It was clear she had no desire to see the man now. He hoped she would play along. Under normal circumstances, he would have no qualms about taking on both of these punks, but she threw a wrench in his plans.

Luckily for them both, Coco didn't have a reputation for being the smartest gangster in town. Tough as nails, yes. Smart? Not so much. That gave Barrett hope that he'd buy the story.

"Where you been, homegirl?" Coco said as he pulled Lottie in a side hug.

"Oh, here and there." Lottie snaked out of Coco's embrace.

"You and her are meeting?" Coco's heavy-lidded gaze traveled from her head to her toes before his lips edged up at the corners. "I see."

Lottie's spine stiffened.

Big Levi, who Barrett knew as the brains of the bunch, elbowed past Coco. He rested his hand on the butt of his gun and pinned Lottie with his gaze. "Who do you work for?"

Lottie folded her arms and gaped at Big Levi, seeming to size him up. "None of your business is who."

Laughter charged from Big Levi, and he took his hand off his weapon. He clapped her shoulder. "You're alright, lady. What's your name again?"

She raised a brow. "Lottie. What's yours?"

Big Levi took a step closer to Lottie. "I go by Big Levi, but you can call me Levi."

"That's good to know."

Barrett nearly rolled his eyes. She had no idea how much danger they were in. Both men were armed and could be extremely dangerous. Yet here she stood, making polite conversation like they were at tea. Although he had to admit she did seem tougher than he initially gave her credit for. That and the fact that she hadn't called him out made him like her a little more than he should.

But what to do with her? She knew Coco. Was she trying to set Barrett up? That didn't seem to be the case. Coco's surprise at seeing Lottie appeared to be genuine. Not to mention her shock at seeing Coco couldn't have been acted out better by Julia Roberts.

Barrett glanced at Lottie before blocking Big Levi from getting any closer. He didn't react to the faint bruises on her face. She must be running from an abusive husband or something. Whatever she had going on, she sure didn't need to be caught up in this. "Like I said, she's with me."

Seconds ticked by as Barrett and Big Levi stared one another down.

Coco cleared his throat. "Look here, we need to get down to business." He eyed Lottie. "I have a feeling we'll see each other soon, but for now, you gotta go."

Barrett dug his room key out of his pocket and handed it to Lottie. "Go on to the room. I'll be there shortly." His eyes implored her not to argue.

She paused a second before taking the key. She glanced at the old-school silver key on a white key-chain with a red-lettered 119 on it before meeting his gaze. Her compassionate yet bewitching hazel eyes seemed to hide a lot of hurt. Although now was not the time, he briefly wondered what she'd been through.

She leaned into his ear. "I'm going to trust you. Just know I have pepper spray."

He grinned, brushing his lips across her forehead like they shared a secret. Coco let out a cat call.

She tensed before glancing at Big Levi. "I hope you all have a good night."

Big Levi beamed at Lottie. "You, too." They all watched her disappear around the side of the hotel before Big Levi turned to Barrett. "You're one lucky dude."

Barrett shrugged. Big Levi had no idea how true that statement was at the moment. His shoulders relaxed as soon as they could no longer see Lottie. He turned to Coco. "I thought the boss wanted to meet me."

"The boss is busy," Coco said, narrowing his eyes. "Don't you own a bed and breakfast or something? Why are you here with a woman?"

Barrett leaned against his Camaro, propping his foot on the tire. "I can't take Lottie there."

Coco nodded. "I guess that makes sense." He sucked air through his teeth. "We have a job for you soon."

A muscle in Barrett's jaw ticked. "I told you I wanted to meet the boss first."

"Ain't gonna happen." Coco shrugged. "You do this job, then I'll make sure you meet the boss."

"What's the job?"

"It don't work like that. You gotta be patient. This ain't some country club where you buy your way in."

"I'm just trying to make some easy money," Barrett said, scratching the back of his neck. "My bed and breakfast isn't bringing in enough for my lifestyle. I already told you I'm not afraid to get my hands dirty."

"You'll be contacted in a few days." Coco turned to walk away. He paused. "Make sure the broad is with you next time we meet."

His spine clenched as he locked his gaze with Coco's. "Lottie has no part in this."

"She does now. With her, you can prove yourself. Without her, the deal is off." Coco smirked. He nodded toward the expedition.

Big Levi saluted Barrett. They climbed inside and sped away.

Barrett breathed in gassy fumes as he stood there in shock. Coco had lost his ever-loving mind.

May as well get this over with. He cracked his knuckles and strode around the building. How would he get this strange woman to help him? But if she agreed, how could he put her in danger and live with himself? He didn't even know her. But Coco did.

What if she was there to check his story? He admitted she seemed tougher than the average woman, but there was no way she'd be able to handle herself with a bunch of criminals. He still wasn't sure she wasn't on their side. Getting her involved could turn out disastrous. He would have to figure something else out.

When he reached his room, he paused. The door had been propped open a crack. He took a deep breath and pushed it open.

Lottie sat in the chair in the corner of the room. With his 9-millimeter luger aimed directly at his head.

Chapter 7

Lottie stood, careful to keep the gun steady. "I don't know what game you and your friends are trying to play, but I ain't the one to mess with."

Barrett raised his hands. If she didn't know better, she'd swear a flash of amusement crossed his features. "No game. I promise."

"If anyone else walks through that door, I will put a bullet between your eyes."

"I have no doubt you will." He bit his bottom lip like he was contemplating something important.

"Go ahead and try something. Just know I'm feeling jumpy, and I'd hate for my finger to slip on the trigger."

He nodded slowly. "I promise I'm not going to hurt you," he said.

"You've got that right," she replied, her tone sharp and distrustful.

"The men from earlier are dangerous. Can you tell me how you know them?" He asked as if he wanted to understand the situation better.

"That's none of your concern," she replied. He was the one meeting them, not her.

"How can I trust you?" he pressed, skepticism threading through his words.

"That's funny," she said with a bitter laugh. "I'm the one who needs to be convinced I can trust you—not the other way around."

"Are we at an impasse here?"

"No," she replied, her voice steady but weary. "I have nothing to do with whatever trouble you're caught up in. I just want to rest. I witnessed a little boy almost drown today, and I'm exhausted."

Her eyes reflected the weight of her experience, and for a moment, the barriers between them softened as he cocked his head. "That's odd. My nephew almost drowned on the beach today. Thank goodness a lady was there to pull him out of the water."

Lottie's stomach clenched. "What is your nephew's name?"

"Brayden. Why?"

"This is crazy," Lottie said, lowering the gun slightly. "Is your sister named Samantha?"

"Yes." His eyes doubled in size. "Are you the woman who saved his life?"

She waved a hand, her cheeks heating. "I was in the right place at the right time. Wow. I never would've thought a person like her would have a druggie brother."

Laughter flowed from his chest. "You'd be surprised."

"I'm leaving." She handed Barrett the gun and then opened the door.

"You'll undo a lot of work and possibly put us both in danger if you leave too soon."

Lottie paused in the doorway. Her gaze landed on the Expedition sitting on the other side of a Ford Bronco. Coco sat in the driver's seat, eating a sandwich.

She turned and smiled. "I'll be right back, honey." She raised her voice a little, not so much to raise suspicion, but enough so Coco could hear. After grabbing a bag out of her Jeep and pulling it around to that side of the hotel, she sauntered toward where Barrett stood. She took a deep breath and leaned close to him. "I hope I don't regret this. Hug me."

Barrett tugged a stray hair away from Lottie's eyes and slipped his arms around her. He buried his face in her hair and whispered, "Thank you."

Still wrapped in each other's arms, they stepped into the dimly lit hotel room. As the door clicked shut, she pushed him away, her eyes filled with determination. "There's no way I'm spending the entire night in this hotel room with you alone."

He nodded. "I agree. I'll arrange for you to have your own room."

Her brow furrowed as she glanced toward the window, worried about their uninvited guest lingering outside. "And what about Snoop out there?"

"We'll just wait until he leaves. It's not a problem," he reassured her, though uncertainty flickered in his gaze as he walked to the sink.

She followed him across the room. "Is that really wise?"

"I can't say for sure, but I'd rather take the risk than put you in danger," he replied, washing his hands.

She sighed, her shoulders heavy with worry. "How do you know Coco?"

"I'd rather not discuss this."

"Are you a drug runner?" Her eyes narrowed as memories of a past life tried to fill her mind.

"No," he said, a flicker of annoyance crossing his features.

"Drug dealer?"

"No." he ran a hand through his messy sandy blonde locks.

Even though she could tell he didn't like her line of questions, she continued. "You got me into this. I feel I deserve some answers."

"It's best if you just leave." His gaze shifted toward the door.

"It seems like it's too late for that."

"You may be right, but I don't owe you any answers," he said, stepping inside the bathroom before poking his head out. "Please excuse me, but I desperately need a shower."

⚓

Within an hour of Coco driving away, Lottie grabbed her purse. She paused momentarily at the hotel door, casting one last lingering glance back at Barrett. He lay slumped on the bed, his tousled hair framing a face that seemed to merge with the dim light of the hotel room. She studied his face carefully—there was something about him that hinted at a hidden depth, an energy that pushed against the label of "everyday druggie."

Lottie had a hunch he was plotting something he wouldn't share with a stranger. Each time she had pressed him with questions, his evasions felt sharper. It was infuriating, to say the least. But what stung was when he closed his eyes and went to sleep during their conversation, leaving her with more questions than she could ask in one sitting. Now that he'd dragged her into his little charade, she felt she had the right to know why.

As she slid into the driver's seat and started the engine, memories surged around her like a tide, pulling her back through the years to her turbulent youth. She could almost hear the echoes of laughter mingling with whispers of mischief. Coco had been a pull for Lottie from the start. Even in his teen years, he had the kind of impulsive spirit that made every day feel like an adventure.

Their first meeting at the Children's Home had been innocent enough, but they quickly bonded over shared moments of rebellion. They would sneak off to the edges of the sprawling grounds, giggling as they pulled out cheap bottles of Boone's

Farm wine that someone he knew hid for them. She remembered savoring the sweet, fruity taste as if it might offer them a hint of freedom.

After they ran away together, he became someone who always had a ready supply of Strawberry Hill and a cigar dangling from his lips, just one more emblem of his reckless bravado. "I'm going big time," he had told her, his eyes bright with ambition and delusion.

Then came the offer that changed her life. Coco had pulled out his stash and, with a cocky grin, suggested she try meth with him. The thrill of it had tempted her. It seemed to promise a high that mirrored the excitement of their escape from their troubled pasts. That's what started Lottie's addiction to meth, among other things.

Now, in the quiet of her car, she couldn't help but shake her head at the sheer foolishness of her choices. The path she had taken alongside Coco had been paved with poor decisions and fleeting highs, and here she was, lost in the very disillusionment she had tried to escape. The weight of that realization settled heavily on her, and as she drove away, the darkness swallowed both the hotel and the memories lingering in her mind.

She'd sleep in her car and decide for sure if she could deal with rehab the following morning. It was either that or disappear. It's not like anyone would care.

Chapter 8

THEN: 1998

With a groan, Lottie admitted that running away from the Children's Home had not been her brightest moment. Her eyes scanned the house Coco had brought her to, and she sighed. Expensive furniture and paintings surrounded her. She'd never felt so out of place in her life. Not even at the Children's Home.

Her stomach gurgled and growled, seeming to agree with her. She covered her tummy, praying no one heard it. How embarrassing.

Coco Flores took a swig of Strawberry Hill and landed a lopsided grin on Lottie. "Yo, I think my cuz has some pimento cheese if you want a sandwich."

Even with patches of heat traveling up her neck, she nodded. She was what most considered heavyset. Food was important. She hadn't considered that when she agreed to leave Pensacola for Alabama.

How would she feed herself? All she'd considered was how cute Coco was, and she couldn't believe he'd asked her to leave with him.

The moment she'd piled into the tricked-out Honda Civic that morning, dread overtook her body. It had never left. She just wanted to show Helen that she didn't need her. Since Helen started dating Larry Kingston, she'd turned into a different person. Their sisterly bond diminished, and Lottie took a back seat. She no longer whispered her secrets to Lottie. Nope. It was all about Larry now. Jealousy burned Lottie's insides, replacing the hunger she'd felt moments before.

The feelings intensified when Coco draped his arm around a brunette's slim shoulders. He moved her highlighted blonde hair away from her face and kissed her throat. Lottie swallowed and looked away. She'd never hated anyone as much as she hated that girl in that moment. Not even Larry Kingston.

She never would've left Pensacola if she'd known Coco planned to pick a girl up on the way to Jackson. Why would Coco want Lottie to come along if he already had a girlfriend? It made no sense.

Surely, he didn't think she'd date Frosty Corbitt. He was like at least twenty-five. Gorgeous but way too old for Lottie since she'd only recently turned sixteen. Her gaze drifted to Frosty. He stood near the fireplace, his thoughts seeming to be lost in the gas flames. His muscles stretched against his white tank top as he rubbed the back of his neck.

A snowman tattoo started at his shoulder and covered the bulk of his forearm. Fitting since his name was Frosty. As she continued to scope him out, she decided she'd never seen someone so fit in her life. His muscles had muscles.

Frosty swiveled around and sauntered over to Lottie. He ran his hand down her face. "What's up, Chica?" He was not Hispanic, so Lottie wondered why he called her Chica. No telling.

"Nothin." She shrugged.

He claimed a seat on the end of the black leather sofa and looked from Lottie to Coco. "I want you both to know you're welcome to stay here for as long as you need."

Coco grinned. "Thank you, cuz." Even though Coco called Frosty his cousin, they weren't related by blood. One look told you that much. Coco had beautiful tan skin, short dark hair, and eyes that could talk women into nearly anything. Frosty's butterscotch locks fell close to his shoulders, and though his artificially tanned skin worked for him, you could tell it was fake.

"No problem," he said, tapping his chin. "How do you plan to earn money?"

"We gonna look for jobs."

"I just so happen to have a couple of openings if y'all are interested."

Lottie's eyes lit up as hope swirled in her chest.

Frosty stood and put his hand out to Lottie. "Coco was kidding about the pimento cheese. Come with me, and I'll make you a ham and cheese sandwich.

After that, I'll show you how to get geared up Frosty style."

Lottie now knew that geared up meant getting high. Little butterflies tickled her insides as she put her hand in Frosty's. Maybe he wasn't too old after all.

Chapter 9

The Next Chapter Rehab was not what Lottie expected at all. She leaned against the steering wheel and stared at the light blue Victorian-style home. It looked like a prop from *"Gone with the Wind."*

When she thought of rehabs, she figured they'd be sterile hospital-type buildings. If not for the big sign, she'd think she was at the wrong address.

She eased into a parking spot at the back of the rehab and quickly approached the entrance. If she didn't hurry, she might lose her nerve. After taking a deep breath, she walked inside the front door.

A plump lady behind a large circular desk greeted Lottie. She looked at Lottie over the rim of her glasses. "Hello. May I help you?"

"Um, yes." Lottie wrung her hands. "I need to see about checking in."

The receptionist lifted her gaze to meet Lottie's. "All right. Do you have a referral?"

"A what? No, I just want to get some help."

She softened her tone. "What's your name, hon?"

"Lottie McKenna," she replied, her voice trembling slightly as she waited for yet another rejection.

"One second." She picked up the desk phone and pushed a button. "We have a Miss McKenna here asking to check in." She paused, listening to what the person at the end of the line said.

Lottie's gaze drifted around the room. Outside a bay window stood a gazebo and several picnic tables. A rocky waterfall flowed, giving Lottie courage. She didn't want to ask for Samantha Silverton, but she may have to.

The woman on Lottie's mind exited the door closest to the bay window. "It's so nice to see you again," Samantha Silverton said as she extended her hand. "Let's chat in my office."

Lottie shook Samantha's hand. "Okay."

Once inside the office, Samantha stepped around the white desk in front of a row of bookcases. "Have a seat," she said, lowering herself into a black leather office chair. "This is a pleasant surprise. What brings you by?"

The scent of lavender permeated the air. Lottie breathed in the calming aroma, claiming one of two blue wingback chairs. "Well, I thought about what you said and think you could help me."

"I'm happy to help you." Samantha nodded, leaning her elbow on her desk. "There's nothing I can do to repay you for saving my boy's life."

Lottie swallowed past the dryness in her throat. "You don't need to repay me, Mrs. Silverton. I believe I was there at the right time for a reason. Actually, more than one."

"Please, call me Samantha. I agree that you were there at the most perfect time," she said with a smile that reached her eyes. "But I do owe you, so how can I help?"

Lottie took a deep breath. "I started using drugs as a teenager. I've been clean for a year now, but I was recently slipped some drugs at my ex-boyfriend's house."

Samantha's brown eyes oozed compassion. Without them, Lottie would've chickened out and run off. Telling her story caused an ache to settle in her stomach.

After Lottie shared some of the sordid details of her past, Samantha cocked her head and met Lottie's gaze. "Do you want to take drugs now?"

"Not so much, but I'm afraid I'm going to relapse. My daughter hates me. Heck, I hate myself some days. After meeting you I got to thinking about how a rehab may be where I need to be."

"I agree, but I'm sorry." Her lips tugged downward, matching the crease in her forehead. "The rehab is full."

Tears welled in Lottie's eyes. She took a deep breath and pushed herself to her feet. "That's okay," she replied softly, her voice wavering. "I showed up unannounced."

Samantha picked up a pencil and tapped her chin gently as she seemed to consider her words. "Please, sit down. I may have another solution."

"What do you mean?" Lottie asked, swallowing past the tears.

"How would you feel about a part-time, temporary position at a bed and breakfast?" Samantha gestured for Lottie to sit.

After reclaiming the seat, Lottie cocked her head slightly. "Doing what?"

"Stocking and cleaning rooms and handling some desk duties. It's not too demanding and would give you plenty of time to enroll in our half-day program."

"I'm not opposed to it." Lottie felt that Samantha Silverton might be the answer to prayers.

But she'd also thought Frosty Corbitt had been all those years ago.

"You'd be helping us out big time. One of our employees had an accident last week, and we've been scrambling to fill her spot."

"Okay. Only if you're sure about this." Lottie bit the side of her lip. "You don't even know me."

"I know enough." With a smile, Samantha leaned into her chair. "How does fifteen an hour, a room at the bed and breakfast, and the program here included in your pay sound?"

"Sounds like it's too much." Lottie shook her head. She had no intention of being a charity case. "I know you own this place. Do you also own the bed and breakfast?"

"My brother and I are partners."

"Really? How many brothers do you have?"

"Just one." Sounded from the doorway.

"Here he is now," Samantha said as she stood.

A shiver traveled down Lottie's spine, and her shoulders stiffened as she slowly turned to face the newcomer.

The frustrating man from the hotel leaned casually against the doorframe, a playful grin plastered across his handsome face.

Lottie's brow furrowed as she narrowed her eyes.

"Hello again, Miss McKenna," he said, his voice smooth and teasing as if their previous encounter had been nothing but a delightful game.

Chapter 10

Barrett couldn't believe the woman he'd spent most of the morning searching for sat in his sister's office.

She landed a hostile gaze on him. "What are you doing here?"

Under different circumstances, he'd tell her that her eyes were lovely. But considering she thought him a drug addict, he better pass on any unwelcome compliments. "Among other things, I'm a patient."

"A patient?"

"Yes. So, I heard the offer Samantha made, and I agree. I'd love to put you to work."

Lottie's brows pinched together. "I don't know about this."

Samantha raised her hand. "I'm confused. You two know each other?"

"We met last night." Barrett grinned. "Kinda a weird situation."

"Is there something I need to know?" Samantha glanced at her watch. "I feel like there's a story here, but we'll have to pick this conversation up in a bit. We have guests coming."

"Who?" Barrett's spine tensed.

Samantha landed worried yet hopeful eyes on Barrett. "Have you met the new preacher from Oak Grove church of Christ?"

"I can't say that I have." His lips pressed together as he planned an escape.

"I'd love it if you both would join us," Samantha said, pleading in her voice.

Barrett gritted his teeth. Samantha should know better than to ask him for a Bible study.

Lottie spoke before he could tell Samantha where she could take that invitation. "I guess that would be okay."

He shut his mouth, shrugging as he met Samantha's shocked gaze. As soon as they entered the breakroom, Lottie bounded across the room and hugged a woman Barrett didn't recognize.

"Sylvia, Alvin, I can't believe you're here."

"Lottie, it's so good to see you, " the man said, a warm smile covering his face.

"Alvin is preaching at Oak Grove now." The woman, who looked like a mixture of Halle Berry and Pocahontas from the cartoon his niece had recently forced him to watch, kept Lottie's hand in hers. "This will be our second week coming here for a study."

Barrett stuck his hand out. "I'm Barrett Donahue. Nice to meet you."

"Alvin Griffin. It's a pleasure to meet you as well."

Barrett joined four other rehab guests at a table while three more positioned themselves at another. He smiled when Lottie sat with the others. The lovely lady appeared to want to keep her distance. He couldn't fault her for that.

"Hi everyone. For those I haven't yet met, I'm Alvin Griffin, and I have been serving as the preacher at Oak Grove for the past three months."

After exchanging greetings, Alvin opened his Bible. "Is there anything you wish you hadn't run from? There are many things in my life, but today we'll talk about the day I went up against an irate dog." Alvin said before pressing his lips together and nodding his head.

"When I was a boy, my parents and I searched for treasures at the junkyard a few miles from our house. I wandered down the dirt road one day and found a blue calculator. After a few minutes, I felt like I needed to get up and run as fast as possible. That's when I noticed a large dog charging at me. I ran as fast as I could, feeling fear trickle down my spine as the dog chased me."

That earned a few gasps from around the tables.

"Dad looked up as I screamed and ran toward the car. He rushed over, opened the back door, and shouted for me to jump in. Just in time, I leaped in before he slammed the door shut, narrowly escaping the dog. The dog, determined to get to me, tried to jump through the partially rolled-down window. I was so grateful I hadn't rolled it all the way down! I heard WHALLUP sounds, and the dog gave up and ran off before long."

"The WHALLUP sounds came from my father hitting the dog with his leather belt, trying to get her to leave me alone. She had me in her sights and was determined to get to me. I was grateful she didn't catch me! Running from that dog felt like a race for my life, as she could have seriously harmed or even killed me. It was an important escape for my safety!"

"Today, there is another race set before me. Set before you. It is the race for our spiritual safety."

That got Barrett's attention.

"Do you realize that Satan is coming for you? Like that dog was determined to get at me, Satan is determined to get at you. At me. At every living soul. Turn with me to 1 Peter 5:8."

"Be sober, be vigilant; because your adversary the devil walks about like a roaring lion, seeking whom he may devour."

"Have you ever looked up the definition of devour? I have. One definition from Merriam-Webster is to eat up greedily or ravenously. I don't like the thought of the word devour pertaining to Satan and me in any way, shape, or form. No sir."

An older gentleman leaned his elbows on the table and looked at Alvin with wide eyes. "Me, neither."

Alvin nodded at the man before continuing. "Satan encourages us to prioritize self, fostering desires that lead us away from God. The lust of the flesh seeks what isn't rightfully ours, while the lust of the eyes values worldly possessions over our spiritual well-being. The pride of life craves recognition and glory, often hindering repentance. The devil thrives on these distractions."

"When I was fleeing that dog, Dad helped me find safety. Today, we have help from Jesus Christ, the Son of God, to protect us from the devil. The Bible provides clear instructions on how to stay safe. Just as I had to follow my dad's directions to get in the car, we must follow the guidance in the Bible to find our way."

A text came through Barrett's phone.

> *I'm ready to meet with you and Lottie. Will send more info tomorrow.*

Barrett inwardly groaned. He had no desire to ask Lottie McKenna for help. There had to be another way.

He stared at the text for another minute before deciding how to reply.

> *Lottie and I are not dating.*

Coco left the message unread. Figures. Barrett turned his attention to the preacher, almost sad that he'd missed part of the lesson.

"Don't you think we are all running from something?" one of the patients asked.

Alvin nodded. "I believe at some point in our lives, we all run from something." He locked his gaze on Barrett's. "Even if we don't want to admit it."

Chapter 11

After filling out paperwork with Samantha, Lottie drove the two miles to the bed and breakfast in the heart of Destin, Florida. She leaned closer to the Jeep window to catch a better glimpse of the stunning scene before her. The two-story home stood majestically, its exterior cloaked in rich red brick, creating a welcoming atmosphere.

The architecture was a delightful mix of history and charm, with intricate details adorning the façade. A graceful wraparound porch embraced the house, with ornate white railings that twirled elegantly, leading down to inviting steps. The overall picture was one of warmth and inviting comfort, a true testament to classic craftsmanship.

A sense of awe washed over her as she pushed the deep brown double doors open. The moment she stepped inside, her eyes widened. The lingering aroma of freshly baked cinnamon muffins filled the room and made Lottie smile. Her stomach rumbled as she continued inside.

Towering ceilings soared high above, adorned with intricate crown molding that added a touch of sophistication. The polished hardwood floors gleamed in the warm light, reflecting the beauty of the refined woodwork that embellished every corner of the space.

At the center of the foyer, a grand staircase captured her attention with its sweeping curves and finely crafted banister, made from dark, rich wood and detailed with ornate carvings. The shiny wood stairs invited her to explore the upper levels. At the same time, elegance and luxury enveloped her, making her feel like she had entered a different world.

It was hard to believe she'd be staying there.

In the room, stood a man with spiky hair so white and thin you could almost see his scalp. "You must be Lottie McKenna," he peered at Lottie. "I'm Douglas Michaelson."

"Yes, hello, Mr. Michaelson."

"Call me Douglas. Follow me, and I'll introduce you to my wife, Mildred."

Lottie stepped behind Douglas, feeling small, considering her head fell below his shoulder. He went behind the lavish wood counter and through the door, stopping in front of a plump woman in a mauve recliner. "Mildred, this is Lottie McKenna."

Mildred's eyes snapped at Lottie. "You may address me as Mrs. Michaelson."

"Good afternoon, Mrs. Michaelson."

Mrs. Michaelson nodded before turning her attention to Wheel of Fortune playing on the television. "I hope Barrett knows what he's doing."

Lottie hoped so, too.

Douglas lowered his gaze and motioned for Lottie to exit. As the door eased shut behind them, he sighed. "Please excuse my Mildred. After falling down the stairs, she's having back spasms and can hardly walk."

"I understand," Lottie said as her eyes landed on the hundred-year-old cash register. "This is beautiful."

"Why don't I show you to your suite so you can get settled?" His eyes crinkled as he smiled.

"I appreciate that."

Once inside her room upstairs, she turned in a circle, taking it all in. Cozy charm oozed from every corner of the space. Who was Barrett Donahue, really? A druggie? She'd never known someone hooked on drugs like him. Maybe he was the dealer and only used occasionally. But why was he in rehab? So many questions.

She shook her head as she lowered herself onto the four-poster bed. Maybe it would be better for her to worry about her own problems.

On impulse, she dialed Rhnae's number. It went straight to voicemail. "Hi, Rhnae. I just wanted to say I love you, and I'm sorry. For everything."

Was the fight worth it? When she'd been on alcohol and drugs, she could let her worries go. Nothing mattered. All she had to do was find Coco. She was sure he'd sell her something that would help her sleep.

No. No. No.

No matter what, she needed to stay strong. How would she win Rhnae's trust if she got back on drugs?

A little voice whispered that a low-dose Valium would help her. Nobody would have to know. She could sleep and wake up refreshed. She pushed the thought away as her phone buzzed with an incoming call from Frankie.

"Hi, Frankie."

"Hey, Aunt Lottie. How are you?"

"Doing better. I tried to call Rhnae."

"I saw that. She's with Simon and Vandon at the movies. Left her phone here by mistake, I guess."

After Lottie filled Frankie in on her new circumstances, she hung up and took a moment to wash her face, splashing cool water on her skin to help keep the earlier thoughts about Valium away. With a deep breath, she strolled down the staircase. Just as Barrett burst through the front door.

Their eyes locked, electrifying the air around her. "Are you following me?"

The smile that had danced across his lips faded, replaced by a frown tugging at the corners of his mouth. "I most certainly am not."

"Then what are you doing here?" She peered at Barrett, dreading his answer.

"Lady, I live here," Barrett said, his irritation evident as he shoved past Lottie, making a beeline toward the back of the room.

She turned on her heel and followed him. "You live here?"

He stopped so abruptly that she nearly collided with him. He grabbed her arm, steadying her. Stormy eyes locked onto hers, piercing her with an intensity that sent shivers down her spine. "That's what I said."

Lottie fought to break free from the magnetic hold of his stare. "Who are you? Really?" she asked in a soft voice.

"A complicated man who needs no more drama." He pinched his eyes closed for a fleeting moment as if her presence pained him. "Would you do me a favor and just do the job Samantha hired you for and leave me alone?"

His words ignited a fire in her belly that licked at her insides like a lollipop. She spoke through gritted teeth as she shrugged free of his grip. "Nothing would make me happier. But I expect you to do the same."

Chapter 12

A little after midnight, Lottie opened the refrigerator and scanned the contents. After Barrett's little episode last night, Douglas showed Lottie around and told her what he needed from her. He and his wife usually ran the place with another part-time employee. After his wife broke her leg, he'd been short-handed. Lottie would work a few hours a day when the other employee was off.

She poured a glass of apple juice and headed toward the stairs. She froze in place as Barrett's voice flowed underneath the bottom of the door. "I told you, Alyssa is not my problem."

He paused a moment. He must be on the phone. "Yes, I realize it's been three years." He raised his voice only to lower it. "Samantha is not to blame."

Lottie had no business standing there listening to a private conversation. But what did he mean by Samantha is not to blame? To blame for what?

Her feet remained glued to the floor. She had to know what she had gotten herself caught up in this time. Seemed she had a knack for finding trouble.

"She was only at the rehab two weeks before she disappeared."

Another pause. "Samantha is not a prison warden. People who check into the rehab are not locked up."

Another pause, and then Barrett barked out a bitter-sounding laugh. "Yes, I know who you are, but you obviously have forgotten who I am. Do you need to be reminded what I'm capable of?"

With a racing heart, Lottie tiptoed upstairs. As soon as she locked the door, she pulled up the internet on her phone. She thought for a moment before deciding what to type.

Daughter of oil tycoon missing from Next Chapter Rehab in Destin... *Alyssa Blankenship, 27, was reported missing by her father James Blankenship. Mr. Blankenship, the CEO of Blankenship Oil believes someone talked her into leaving the rehab. Mr. Blankenship is offering a $50,000 reward for information leading to Alyssa's safe return.*

Interesting. It appeared that Alyssa Blankenship was an addict. Lottie guessed even the wealthy could get addicted.

The next headline took a different, more deadly tone.

> ***Chadwick Jennings found dead ... last place seen Next Chapter...****Chadwick Jennings, 44, was reported missing by his girlfriend after he checked out of Next Chapter Rehab last week. His body was found near the marker of highway 10 late last night by a man who stopped to change his flat tire.*

That poor man. How were these two people connected to Barrett? Was he in on it? The next story caused even more questions.

> ***An anonymous tip leads to Alyssa Blankenship in Mobile, Alabama...*** *After three months missing, Alyssa Blankenship was found at a beach house in Mobile. She said she needed time alone and that no one coerced her to run away.*

Lottie shuddered. Something definitely seemed off at that rehab. Yet, she struggled to accept that Samantha could be linked to anything shady.

Maybe she should go home and forget about rehab. She would, but Pensacola felt like a distant memory, a place too fraught with her past mistakes to be a refuge. She knew she couldn't return until she had proven to Rhnae that she was a changed woman who deserved a second chance. Her unresolved issues loomed large, and the prospect of facing Rhnae again felt too much to bear. The thought of leaving without a plan gnawed at her, and she wrestled with the uncertainty of her next steps.

Her head pounded relentlessly as she contemplated her next move. Fueled by determination, she pushed herself up and quickly surveyed her dimly lit room. Her gaze fell upon the nearest chair—a sturdy wooden piece marked with scratches that held their own tales. Though she sensed no immediate danger, she seized the chair and dragged it across the creaking floor. She positioned it firmly under the doorknob, wedging it tightly to prevent anyone from entering. She had done this countless times over the years during her stays with Rhnae at shabby motels and people's houses she didn't know. That chair offered her a sense of comfort, connecting her a bit more to her daughter.

As her eyes grew heavy, she decided the stress of the past two weeks was making her overreact. She would do her job at the bed and breakfast and try to get better. She'd also keep her distance from Barrett and his bizarre dealings.

Barrett stood outside Lottie's bedroom door, listening to her soft snores. Someone had been outside his office when he was on the phone with James Blankenship.

Had it been Lottie eavesdropping? Or another guest? Had his instincts been off when he determined she was not a threat? He'd been wrong before.

There had been a time when he would've sworn Alyssa would die before taking drugs. Before becoming involved with criminals. She had proved him wrong. And he would not allow another woman to make a fool out of him.

Never again.

Chapter 13

At five am, Lottie bolted out of bed and straight to the shower. Forty minutes later, she dragged the chair away from the door and headed downstairs for her morning shift at six.

Douglas glanced at her over the rim of his glasses. "Morning, Lottie." He said as he pulled the glasses off. "How'd you sleep?"

Terrible. "The bed was so comfortable," Lottie said, focusing on the positive.

"That's good to hear." He pointed at the kitchen. "Grab you some breakfast before your shift."

"Don't mind if I do." She glanced toward Barrett's office on the way by. The door was closed tight. He was probably asleep.

After a hearty breakfast of scrambled eggs, biscuits, and gravy, Lottie waddled to the front desk area, patting her tummy. "That was delicious."

Douglas grinned. "My cooking can't compare to Mildred's, but I'm glad you enjoyed it."

"I did."

"Good. I figured I'd spend the first couple of hours letting you shadow me, and then I'll shadow you. How does that sound?"

"Works for me."

Four hours later, Lottie had successfully checked two guests out, cleaned the kitchen, checked a guest in, and balanced the register.

A stocky bald man with a graying beard entered. Before Lottie greeted him, Douglas let her know he was the other employee. "How was your first day?"

"Not too bad. How has your day been?"

"Good. I'm Howie, by the way."

As it turned out, Howie was a church member where Alvin preached. What a small world, Lottie thought as she drove to the rehab.

After her first session with a kind counselor, she left with a smaller weight on her chest.

She sat at an empty table in the break area, bit her lip, and glanced at the phone. Before she chickened out, she typed a text to Rhnae.

I love you.

Knots coiled in her stomach as she stared at the phone, waiting for any sign of hope from Rhnae.

She pressed on her side as a cry rose within. Rhnae wanted to talk!

Rhnae loved the message. As Lottie sat the phone on the table, pure joy emanated from her. She glanced around the room, only to lock gazes with Barrett.

He picked his way toward her table. "I believe that's the first time I've seen you smile. You must've got some good news."

Not even Barrett's brooding presence could cast a shadow over her elated mood. "I did."

"Did your first session go well?" he inquired, tilting his head as if trying to figure out what made her smile.

"I'd guess better than yours since you're still hanging around with druggies." She closed her eyes for a moment as shame for her words threatened to overtake her. Why had she said that?

A frown tugged at his lips, and fire laced his tone. "What's that supposed to mean?"

Even though she needed to be nice, it seemed this man brought out the worst in her. "I'm just curious why you meet thugs at cheap motels when you own a bed and breakfast? Never mind, you'd never bring someone like Coco there."

A flicker of annoyance crossed his features. "You think you've got everything figured out, right?"

She picked up a magazine about coastal living and rolled it into a cylinder. She needed to keep her hands busy, or she might be tempted to thump Barrett's ears. "It's not like it's hard."

"What about your relationship with Coco?" he pressed, his voice thick with accusation. "You two seemed to know each other very well the other night. Want to tell me about that?"

She sprang to her feet and instantly regretted it. It was difficult to be intimidating when she barely reached the shoulder of the person she wanted to intimidate. She craned her neck. "No, I don't."

He leaned close enough that Lottie could've caressed his smooth jaw. Not that she wanted to. He smiled thinly. But all Lottie noticed was the woodsy cedar fragrance snagging her senses. He smelled like a man ought to smell. She fought the urge to sniff his shirt.

He lifted an eyebrow. "What are you thinking about?"

She squeezed the rolled-up magazine tight. "I want to understand what's happening. If you're involved in anything illegal, please keep me out of it. Do you understand? I have a daughter who means everything to me, and I won't allow you or anyone else to jeopardize our relationship."

He grunted. "I wasn't planning on it."

"Then tell me what's going on." She closed the small space between them, her eyes locked to Barrett's.

Someone cleared their throat, but neither Lottie nor Barrett moved. "What's going on with you two?" Samantha asked. "I can't tell if you got off on the wrong foot or if you're so attracted to each other that you're acting like children."

Samantha's words sent Lottie back a few paces. She moved her gaze to Samantha. "I'm sorry."

"What about you, Barrett? You're thirty-nine years old, yet you're acting like a teenager." Samantha bit her lip as if she were trying to keep from laughing.

His spine visibly relaxed, and he looked contrite. "I am also sorry."

"Good. Are you busy Sunday, Lottie?" Samantha asked, her warm smile directed at a maintenance worker who ambled past, tools clinking softly at his side.

"Not that I know of." Lottie briskly shook her head. "Why do you ask?"

"I wanted to invite you to church." Samantha took a step closer to Lottie, giving her a feeling that she offered true and genuine friendship.

"That's very nice of you. Where do you attend?"

"We go to the church where Alvin preaches," Samantha explained, her voice filled with genuine warmth.

"I should be able to do that." Lottie smiled at Samantha. If only she'd had someone like her as a friend when she was younger.

"How about we pick you up at 9? We only live a few blocks away."

"Sounds good." She glanced at Barrett, who had moved across the room, leaning against the wall, his expression unreadable. "Do you attend there, too?"

Barrett's eyes darkened, and his forehead creased. "I don't go to church anywhere. And don't ask me to either," he replied, his voice sharp as he pushed off the wall and stomped away.

Chapter 14

Sunlight poured in the dining room's bay window. Lottie slathered cream cheese and strawberry jam on toast and sunk her teeth in. She glanced at the clock on the microwave. Thirty minutes later, Samantha and her family would be there to pick her up for church. She found herself looking forward to it. Especially seeing Brayden again.

She still couldn't believe Rhnae was open to talking about their situation. That gave Lottie hope and the will to do everything in her power to be the mother she should be, the person God would have her be.

A commotion coming from the lobby grabbed her attention. With her toast forgotten, she speed-walked toward the lobby.

A red-faced Douglas stood behind the counter, trying to calm down a woman with striking coppery red hair wearing a pale pink silk pajama set. Fancy

clothes meant the woman was probably high maintenance.

"That room you put me in last night smells dirty,"
the woman said.

Lottie had been right. Definitely high maintenance.

"Each of our rooms is thoroughly cleaned between each guest. I promise you that, Miss
Blankenship," Douglas said, his face turning a shade
darker.

Lottie stopped on the other side of the woman.
"Can I help with anything?"

The woman landed light brown eyes on Lottie and
turned away like Lottie was a mere inconvenience.

This suited Lottie just fine, considering her eyes
doubled in size when she recognized the woman as
the same Alyssa Blankenship who had gone missing
from rehab.

The woman lowered her head to look at Mildred
as she entered the room in her wheelchair. "Mildred, I expect my room to be thoroughly cleaned.
I want every inch disinfected before I go back in
there."

Mildred landed her gaze on Lottie. "Did you clean
Miss Blankenship's room?"

"What's the room number?" Lottie cocked her
head. "I have only cleaned one room since I just
started yesterday."

"Room 112," Douglas said, cutting his wife off by
raising his finger.

"No, that's not the room I cleaned."

"Don't be making excuses. It's your responsibility to clean every room up to our high standards." Mildred pointed her finger at Lottie.

Lottie's spine stiffened, and if not for needing to get through this rehab for Rhnae, she would've told Mildred where to stick her high standards. Instead, she cut her gaze at Douglas, who looked embarrassed. "I can clean the room now."

Alyssa grabbed her purple Louis Vuitton bag off the counter. "I'll be back in an hour. My room better be clean."

"You heard her," Mildred said before wheeling into her room.

Douglas pressed his lips together and sighed. "Sorry about that. My Mildred isn't usually so hard to deal with. I think her leg is hurting her."

Even though Douglas tried to make excuses for his wife's behavior, it wasn't his fault. Lottie faintly smiled. "I better get busy."

After calling Samantha to tell her she'd drive herself and come late, she threw on a sweatsuit and let herself inside the room. The decorations could've come straight from a scene from Gone With the Wind. As she stared around the room, she considered her situation could be way worse.

Thirty minutes later, Lottie ran the vacuum under the four-poster bed. She hit something hard, and it stuck in the vacuum. A jump drive. Odd. She doubted it belonged to Alyssa Blankenship. And that woman would throw an ever-loving fit if she found it. With a shrug, Lottie slipped it inside her pocket and finished the deep clean.

If she hurried, she could still make it to hear the sermon. As she locked the door and swiveled around, she collided with someone. "I am so sorry."

"Not a problem, ma'am." The man said, amusement dancing in his light blue eyes. "Coco told me he saw you last week, but I never dreamed I'd get lucky enough to run into you."

Oh no. The blood drained from her face. Who was she kidding? More like her entire body. "Frosty?"

"The one and only." He leaned against the wall as his gaze traveled from her head to her toes and back again. He looked like Frosty in the face, but his demeanor was totally different. The old Frosty wore hip-hop clothes and looked like a wannabe rapper. The Frosty standing here now appeared sophisticated and wealthy. Touches of gray peppered through his jet-black hair, giving him an air of sophistication Lottie would've never dreamed he could pull off.

"What are you doing here?"

"I own several car dealerships across Florida and Alabama. Just opened one here, and I'm checking on it."

"Oh. So, you're not dealing?"

"I'm wheeling and dealing cars, baby." He grinned. "How would you like a job? You can come home with me to Key West or stay here."

"Thanks for the offer, but I like what I'm doing here."

He licked his lips and took a step closer to Lottie. "You're too pretty to be a cleaning lady."

"That's your opinion," Lottie said as she stepped back. "Have a good day, Frosty." She turned to walk away.

He grabbed her arm. "I'll make things worth your while. I promise."

A screeching voice interrupted their conversation. "My room better be clean." Alyssa Blankenship elbowed her way in between Lottie and Frosty.

As Frosty watched Alyssa disappear into her room, Lottie ran down the hall before he could see which room was hers.

Chapter 15

Despite Lottie's disappointment that Frosty brought a date to the New Year's Eve party, she planned to enjoy herself. Swaying to Prince's hit song, Party Like It's 1999, she sipped on a strawberry wine cooler. She still couldn't believe it was the last day of 1999. Some people thought the world would end tonight. Lottie didn't think it would, but she wanted to make the best of the night just in case.

She knocked a gold balloon out of her way and leaned against the wall. Frosty had gone all out for this party. Gold and silver balloons and streamers decorated the room, and a Welcome 2000 sign hung on the wall. She peered at Frosty and his latest airheaded blonde bimbo under hooded eyes. Whatever.

Lottie had no clue why Frosty wouldn't give her a chance. He'd initially told her they couldn't be together in public because of the near ten-year age gap. But the airhead was the same age as Lottie, and nobody here would question whether they were a couple. She'd made it public. Way too public if you asked Lottie.

During a lull in the music, the airhead's obnoxious laughter echoed across the room. She glared at Lottie before smiling sweetly at Frosty and wrapping her bony arms around his waist. Her metallic silver minidress rose an inch, nearly exposing her backside. That girl needed to learn how to dress.

Lottie glanced at her blue jean button-up shirt that fell at the waist of her glittery jeans and sighed. She'd lost most of her weight, so what could the problem be? Men found her attractive. Why wasn't she good enough for Frosty?

She finished the wine cooler and headed to the ice chest for her fifth one. After spending the past year working as a drug runner, Frosty said he had big plans for her. She'd thought that meant they would finally make their relationship official. Apparently not.

Working for Frosty meant no more meth, so Lottie had steered clear of that drug, which was a good thing. But sadly, alcohol and pills had become her constant companions when she wasn't on the job.

The airheaded bimbo strutted away from Frosty, her friend tagging behind, headed toward the bathroom.

This would give Lottie a chance to confront her. She needed to know the deal, and Frosty sure wouldn't tell her. The alcohol clouded her mind and gave her a nerve she wouldn't have had otherwise. She stopped outside the door, waiting for the two girls to come out.

"Can you believe that stank girl Lottie thinks she has a chance with my Frosty?" The airhead's voice cut Lottie's nerves worse than fingernails on a chalkboard.

"No, I don't think she does."

"It doesn't matter anyway. Frosty said she would be gone within the next few days."

"Really? Where is she going?"

"Who cares?"

Red clouded Lottie's vision as she marched away from the door, her sights set on Frosty. He would be answering to her.

Coco met Lottie before she reached Frosty and steered her into the nearest bedroom. A man looked from her to Coco before ignoring them for the line of cocaine he had on a mirror.

"What do you think you're doing?" Coco pinned Lottie with his gaze as if the man snorting drugs didn't exist.

"I want to know why Frosty told his latest airhead-ed bimbo I was leaving." Tears tugged at the corners of Lottie's eyes.

Coco glanced at the floor. "Look, I don't know everything. But I was going to tell you to get out of here in the morning."

Her chest tightened. "Why?" She shoved Coco's chest. "Why?"

"His new girl wants you gone." Coco's eyes turned hard. "You better not go out there and say a word. I promise you'll regret it."

"Where will I go, Coco?"

The man stepped in front of Lottie, wiping his nose. "You can come home with me. My parents own a grocery store, and I'll put you to work there."

Lottie checked the man out. He looked slightly like Jared Leto from one of her favorite TV shows, My So-Called Life. A shiver covered her arms. "I don't know about that. Where do you live?"

"I live in Miami, and you'll love it." His lips spread into a grin that set Lottie at ease.

"I think you should go, Lot. This is a perfect solution." Coco said as he looked at the man with appreciation. "What's your name, dude?"

"Eddie," he said, sticking his hand out. "My name is Eddie Chambers."

Chapter 16

As soon as the hallway grew quiet, Lottie left for church. Even though she missed part of the sermon, she wanted to be there.

Once she pulled into the parking lot, she glanced at the tan brick building, and uncertainty crept up her spine. She needed to go inside, but would she ever be good enough to be called a child of God? She closed her eyes, took a breath, and stepped out of her Jeep.

She walked through the foyer as quietly as possible and claimed a seat at the end of a pew in the back row. A woman with kind eyes and short blonde hair smiled at Lottie. She returned the smile before taking a Bible from the back of the pew.

Alvin Griffin, the preacher, flipped through his Bible. "Turn with me to 1 Peter 5:8."

"Be sober, be vigilant; because your adversary the devil walks about like a roaring lion, seeking whom he may devour."

"This means we need to stay alert as the enemy waits for moments of weakness to strike. His tactics vary for each person; for some, he tries to keep them away from encouraging services. As highlighted in Hebrews 10:24, we should encourage one another to love and good works."

He paused and glanced around the auditorium. "Satan understands that keeping you away from church and fellow believers gives him the victory. Some try to persuade others to stop studying the Bible, God's antibiotic against sin. They may claim Bible class is unnecessary."

"Let's read what the Psalmist wrote in chapter 119, verses 10-11."

"With my whole heart I have sought You; Oh, let me not wander from Your commandments! Your word I have hidden in my heart, That I might not sin against You!"

"Now let's go down a few verses to 105."

"Your word is a lamp to my feet And a light to my path."

"Satan will do everything in his power to get us to stay as far away from the Word as possible. He wants us to question God."

"Some ask what's the use? Or why am I in this position?" He scanned the auditorium again. "Many blame God for their struggles. Often, we forget who is in control and capable of all things. We serve the King of Kings!"

"Let's read Luke 22:31 to see what Jesus told Simon that applies to us even today."

"And the Lord said, "Simon, Simon! Indeed, Satan has asked for you, that he may sift you as wheat."

"When we are unaware or distracted, the enemy works, sowing discord while we sleep, as noted in Matthew 13:25. Once he gains a foothold in our lives, he establishes a base of operations, using us against others—brethren, family, and friends. He may lead us away from services, diminish our faithfulness, and destroy our influence."

Lottie crossed her legs and uncrossed them, only to cross them again. She had heard many sermons the past year, so what had her nerves on edge? Memories of her time with Frosty threatened to cut her air off. No. She would not allow her mind to wander. Frosty had no control over her. Not anymore.

She focused on the preacher's deep voice. "I want you to ask yourself if you lack Christ in your heart. Go ahead and think about that for a second. Your answer is very important. Why? Because the Devil easily sets up his base in those who lack Christ in their hearts. From this base, he can achieve his evil aims, rendering individuals useless in the church and destroying their influence among family, friends, and the community. He promotes a worldly lifestyle and hypocrisy, similar to what Paul described in Ephesians 4:19, where individuals surrender to lasciviousness and uncleanness with greed."

Did Lottie lack Christ in her heart? She'd never thought of it like that. For too many years, her life had been about getting high or drunk, no matter the cost. Would Christ even want someone like her? Yes, she could attend service and go through the motions, but would she ever truly be a part of the church?

"He knows where to attack you. So, how might we keep him from getting a place in our lives? First, put up a steadfast defense. Turn with me to 1 Corinthians 15:58."

"Therefore, my beloved brethren, be steadfast, immovable, always abounding in the work of the Lord, knowing that your labor is not in vain in the Lord."

"We must put on the whole armor of God as stated in Ephesians 6:11-12."

"Put on the whole armor of God, that you may be able to stand against the wiles of the devil. For we do not wrestle against flesh and blood, but against principalities, against powers, against the rulers of the darkness of this age, against spiritual hosts of wickedness in the heavenly places."

"We have the means to fend off his attacks. Immerse yourself in the word of God. Hold to your ground. Submit yourselves to God. Resist the devil, and he will flee from you. James 4:7."

With a shudder, Lottie questioned whether she'd truly tried to fend off the devil. Had she made up her mind to change her life or not?

"God provides the necessary equipment to hold our position and give no place to the enemy. With all of this, the devil can certainly make no advancement that we do not allow him to make, and the only place he can get is the one we give him."

The preacher was right. Lottie had a decision to make. But was she strong enough?

Chapter 17

As soon as Lottie's hand touched the door handle, Samantha called her name. "Hey, Lottie."

For a brief second Lottie considered walking through the door like she hadn't heard. She couldn't do it. Instead, she turned. "Hey."

"David and I would love for you to come for lunch."

Lottie looked at Samantha's emerald green suit and silky cream top, feeling like a frumpy mushroom in her brown corduroys and white button-up. "No, I don't want to impose."

"Impose?" Samantha crinkled her forehead. "We want you to come."

David Silverton hugged Lottie. "It's good to see you again. Now that I'm more to my senses I want to thank you for saving Brayden." His eyes misted over as he spoke. "Please come to lunch."

"I'm thankful I was there." Lottie's cheeks heated. She wasn't used to so much attention. Or praise.

On the way to their cars, David's phone dinged. He read the message with a slight frown. "Looks like I'll be grabbing a taco on the way to the nursing home."

"What happened?" Samantha cocked her head.

"Their air went out an hour ago. I need to go see what the problem is." He pecked Samantha on the lips, kissed Brayden and Scarlett, and nodded to Lottie. "Can you give Sam and the kids a ride home?"

Lottie had never been more thankful for a clean, newer model vehicle. "I'd be happy to."

After switching the car seat over, they headed to Samantha's home. Samantha shared that David owned a small heating and air company, and his only employee was off today. This was the first time Lottie had ever driven anyone besides Rhnae anywhere. Her heart picked up its speed. So, this was what it felt like to have a friend. Someone to chat with. To have meals with.

As Lottie eased into the driveway, her eyes widened. With its columns, airy front porch, and light pink color, Samantha's two-story home screamed Southern charm with a beachy twist. The charm ended when she got to the back of the house. Barrett leaned against his Camaro, his blonde hair blowing in the wind.

He raised a brow when Lottie got out of the Jeep. "What's up?"

Even though he looked surprised to see her there, a grin jotted across his lips that sent Lottie's blood into a tizzy. She swallowed to clear the unwelcome emotion.

"Hey. We were just about to have lunch." Samantha sat Brayden down, who promptly sidestepped it over to Barrett and held his arms up. "Wanna join?"

Barrett swung Brayden into his arms. "Sure." He favored Lottie with a stare. "What's on the menu?"

"You'll see," Samantha answered as she walked inside the open-concept home.

Within twenty minutes, they had their plates and were settled at the table—the kids with chicken strips and macaroni and the adults with heaping bowls of savory shrimp and grits.

Samantha sopped up the juice in her bowl with a roll, popped it in her mouth, and pushed her bowl away. She met Lottie's gaze. "We're having a ladies' day next Saturday at church. I'd love for you to come."

"That sounds nice."

"You may know the speaker. Keatyn Griffin from Pensacola."

"Yes, she's the preacher's wife."

"Can I go, mommy?" Scarlett asked with a mouthful of chicken.

"Of course you can." Samantha bunched her mouth up. "You need to swallow your food before speaking, remember."

Brayden chose that moment to throw his spoon across the room. Thank goodness Lottie didn't have to answer the invitation.

Barrett cleared his throat. When Lottie's eyes darted to him, he cast a knowing glance at her. "Did you enjoy your first week at the bed and breakfast?"

Thirty minutes ago, if someone would've asked her if her knees could go all rubbery while she was sitting at a table, she would've said no. But now? Her knees caved in, and she wasn't quite sure how she kept from sliding out of the chair. "It was good. Douglas is a kind man."

"Yes, he and Mildred have worked for our family for around five years." He turned to Scarlett. "What do you say we play a game of HORSE?"

"Okay! I'll get the basketball and meet you out-side."

Samantha stood. "Why don't we all join in? Lottie, I'll grab you some shorts and a T-shirt."

And just like that Lottie was signed up to play basketball with Barrett. She blew her breath out.

Barrett laughed. "You scared I'll make you look bad?"

"Nope." She said as she followed Samantha into the bedroom.

As soon as they started their game, a black Mercedes SUV with dark-tinted windows pulled into the driveway. The driver, who looked like he was head-ing to a black-tie event, jumped out and opened the back door.

Samantha cut her eyes to Barrett before meeting the passenger halfway. "Hello, Uncle Elliott."

"Hello, dear." He replied before landing a disap-proving glance at Lottie. "Who is this?"

Lottie stuck her hand out. "Lottie McKenna, sir. It's a pleasure." She inwardly groaned, figuring she sounded like an idiot. What was a pleasure? Surely not his grim expression or the light brown spots covering his bald head.

When he didn't answer Lottie, Samantha cleared her throat and pasted on a smile. "This is Elliott Jennings, our uncle." Samantha cut a dirty look in his direction.

That name rang a bell, but Lottie couldn't place where she'd heard it.

"I'm here to let you both know I'll be out of the country for a week. Maybe more." He glanced at his shiny Rolex watch. "Barrett, you may be called upon to handle issues with the company should they arise."

"I'll be ready, Uncle Elliott."

"See that you are." He gave a clipped nod before loading back into his car without so much as a goodbye.

Barrett sighed and met Lottie's curious gaze. "Don't ask."

An hour later, sweat poured down Lottie's shirt, and she regretted waking up that morning. But there was no way she'd let Barrett get the ball away from her. They'd escalated to a game of one-on-one after Scarlett tuckered out.

Barrett slapped the ball out of Lottie's arms and ran in the other direction. Fire coursed through her legs as she closed the distance between them. Barrett stopped and turned toward her. Before she could stop herself, she fell into Barrett, and they crashed to the ground.

With a laugh, Barrett lowered his head to the ground while Lottie scrambled to move away from him. He raised a hand and brushed a blonde curl away from her face.

Her muscles froze as his hand lingered on her ear a second longer than he should have. She tensed and fought to her feet.

"Mommy asked me to bring you something to drink," Scarlett announced as she set two glasses of lemonade on the table on the back porch.

"Thank you, sweetie." Barrett landed a smile on Scarlett that took Lottie's breath away.

What was she doing? She couldn't allow herself to fall for a jerk like Barrett. He was involved in no telling what. That's probably how he got the bed and breakfast. Illegal activity and relying on his kind sister and uncle. She needed to stop things from getting any more emotional.

Before it was too late.

Chapter 18

S oft snores came from the sofa, where Brayden had curled up for a nap. With the ladies enjoying the outdoors, Barrett had time to think. Too much time, if you asked him. If he had good sense, he'd keep Lottie McKenna at arm's length. His main concern was figuring out who was behind the uptick in criminal activity down the coast. Because once he found that out, he'd know who killed Chadwick. It had been a few days since he'd heard from Coco. He picked up his phone and sent a text.

I'm ready to meet.

You and Lottie?

Just me. It's now or never.

Instead of texting a reply, Barrett's phone rang. His brow furrowed as he answered with a clipped, "Donahue."

"We have a job, but it won't be easy."

"I didn't expect it would be."

"Keep your phone close. I'll be in touch soon."

As the line went dead, Barrett stared out the window at Scarlett bounding out of the pool while Samantha and Lottie watched from the patio.

He clenched his jaw. Hazel eyes couldn't get in the way of the main objective. Lives could be at stake. Chadwick's death couldn't be in vain. Barrett wouldn't allow it.

His phone buzzed with an incoming call from James Blankenship. Good grief. What could the man want now? "This is Barrett."

"I have good news!" James said, his voice full of enthusiasm.

"What's that?"

"Alyssa called. She's staying at your bed and breakfast. Have you seen her?"

A chill blanketed Barrett's body. "No, I haven't."

"She says she's ready to make everything right."

"I'm happy for you, James. Maybe now we can move on."

"Exactly! Let's plan to have dinner soon. I'll fly you both to Orlando for a few days."

"That's not going to happen, but I am happy for you."

James Blankenship's voice turned hard as steel, all enthusiasm from earlier gone. "Now listen here, my baby girl wants you to come to dinner. I expect you to do whatever it takes to make her happy." The line went dead.

Barrett pressed his lips together, resisting the urge to stomp his phone into a million pieces. James knew that Barrett wasn't one to mess with. Barrett also knew the same for James. One time, James had come at Barrett with fists flying over Barrett not giving Alyssa her way on getting engaged. The only problem was that James had two meatheads with him that also had fists flying.

All three of them learned a lesson that day. The two meatheads ended up in the ER, while James had a private doctor come in and fix his shoulder.

They chose not to press charges.

The back door snapped shut as Scarlett high-tailed it toward her bedroom, dripping water and wrapped in a towel. A smile tugged at his lips.

"I like Lottie and don't want you hurting her." Samantha stood in the doorway, hand on hip.

His gaze darted to the window. Lottie sat in a lounge chair, her head back and hair tumbling to the concrete. He swallowed and met Samantha's fiery gaze. "I don't have anything to do with Lottie."

"Liar," Samantha said, steering Barrett to the cream sectional.

"She's a good-looking woman, but that's the end of it." He claimed the end of the sectional. "I don't plan on getting involved with her."

"You're taking this scarred marine with an attitude persona a bit far when it comes to her," Samantha said, her voice full of concern.

"Don't you understand how important this is?" he shot back.

"Of course I do." Lines creased in her forehead, and she rubbed the bridge of her nose. "I'm the one who asked you to figure out if my rehab is somehow connected to…" she lowered her voice… "criminals."

"I get that, but I sometimes wonder if you fully comprehend how dangerous these people are."

"You and I both know they had Chadwick killed," she continued. "This isn't a game. I know that lives are at stake."

"By the way, Alyssa is staying at the bed and breakfast."

"What? Why didn't you tell me?"

"I didn't know." He closed his eyes. "James just called and demanded I fly out to Orlando with her for a few days."

"Why would you do that?"

"He thinks it'll be good for her."

"Yeah, anything for his precious Alyssa." Samantha's eyes doubled in size. "You're not thinking of getting back together with her, are you?"

"Absolutely not," he said firmly.

"What are you going to do then?" she asked, a hint of worry lacing her voice as she leaned closer, searching his eyes for reassurance.

He took a deep breath. "My job. Figure out who's stealing from the good people along the coast."

"Please be careful. The last thing I want is for you to get hurt."

He let out a short, barking laugh. "Come on, I was a marine, trained for tough situations, and now I'm an undercover detective. Don't worry about me getting hurt. I can manage just fine, big sister."

A sharp gasp echoed from the doorway as Lottie entered the bright, airy room. With a quick flick of her wrist, she pulled a small item from her purse and approached Barrett, her footsteps quiet against the hardwood floor. "I found this in the room of the missing woman," she said, her voice barely above a whisper as if the very act of speaking could summon unwanted attention. "I don't think it belongs to her, so I took it, hoping to keep her from filing a complaint."

With a decisive motion, Lottie dropped a black jump drive into Barrett's lap. She turned to Samantha, gratitude shining in her eyes. "Thank you for your hospitality," she murmured, her tone earnest. Before either of them could respond, she darted out of the house.

Barrett looked at the jump drive before shifting his gaze to Samantha. "I suppose you're not the only one who knows I'm an undercover detective now."

Chapter 19

THEN: 2008

Light flashed in Lottie's peripheral vision. She bolted to the other side of the dumpster, her insides trembling. A chunk of recently dyed, inky black hair fell into her eyes. She wiped the greasy locks away with a bruised hand. Enter Sandman blasted from the Miami nightclub. Usually, she would jam out to this song, but not after her argument with Eddie.

What would make him think she was eyeballing another man? The only reason she'd come out was for him. Why else would she leave her three-month-old baby with his sister? Shannon seemed to adore Rhnae, but it was Lottie's job to take care of her, not Shannon's.

"Ohhhhh, Lottie?" Eddie's singsong voice came from down the alley.

Lottie's heart dropped, and she bolted upright. "Leave me alone, Eddie. I haven't done nothing to you."

"You humiliated me in front of Ozzie," Eddie said as he backhanded her. "After the way you acted, he thinks you've got the hots for him."

Her shoulder bounced into the dumpster before her head hit the brick building. Sharp throbs traveled from her scalp to her torso, and she sobbed. "I swear I didn't mean to."

He grabbed her hair and dragged her to her feet. "I'll teach you not to embarrass me again." He raised his fist.

Lottie closed her eyes, waiting for the blow that would likely knock her out. Flashing blue lights caused Eddie to drop his hand.

A policewoman stepped out of her car. "What's going on?" She put her hand on the weapon strapped to her hip. "Ma'am, are you okay?"

Eddie hugged Lottie closely. "She's drunk as a skunk. Been out here throwing her guts up."

The officer cocked her head, meeting Lottie's gaze. "Is that right?"

"Tell her, honey." Eddie squeezed Lottie's shoulder. If she said anything she may never see Rhnae again. The cops always blamed her anyway. Most of them knew Eddie's family and thought they were good people. They may be, but Eddie was far from good. Just a good actor.

"Yeah, I'm fine." Lottie squeaked, her voice trembling slightly as she wiped a trickle of blood from her nose.

"She fell into the dumpster and hit her head." Eddie barked a laugh as he shook his head back and forth, clicking his tongue. "I swear she gets clumsier every time she drinks."

Even though the officer hesitated, she nodded. "You should get her home."

Eddie flashed a wide grin, regaining his cockiness. "Yeah, I promise to take good care of her at home, Officer." His fingers dug into Lottie's arm as he pulled her to his side. "Good care. Thanks for checking on us."

Chapter 20

Thanks to Lottie's work schedule, Monday morning came early. By ten o'clock, she had cleaned the kitchen, dining area, and foyer and checked a couple from Tennessee out.

She laid the duster behind the counter and took a sip of water. Another hour and she'd have her second session at the rehab. This time, she'd be in a group.

Alyssa Blankenship moved down the stairs and stopped in front of Lottie. Something was on her mind, and Lottie wasn't sure she wanted to know what it was. Maybe her commode needed cleaning with a toothbrush.

Before Alyssa could say anything, the front door swung open. Barrett strutted inside and landed a smile on Lottie that made her heart triple in speed.

Alyssa narrowed her eyes, walked up to Barrett, and kissed his lips. Barrett pushed her away and held her at a distance. She pooched her bottom lip out. "Is that the way to greet your fiancé?"

A shadow fell across his face, and he frowned. "You are not my fiancé."

"Yes, I am. You're just in denial."

"You and I haven't been together in years."

"Well, I'm here to win you back." She caressed the side of his face. "I'm used to getting what I want, Barrett." She said as she walked up the stairs. She paused midway. "Remember that."

That entire interaction made Lottie want to go throw up. *I'm used to getting what I want, Barrett.* Ridiculous.

From the look on Barrett's face, he felt the same way Lottie did. She couldn't help but wonder about their story. What happened between them? Now that she knew Barrett was as far from a criminal as he could get, she wanted to know more. About the case. Not him. The case only.

She used to run from cops. There's no way he'd ever want anything to do with her if he knew her history. Like Eddie used to say, she'd never be good enough for a decent man. What would he want with a drug addict? Nothing. For the hundredth time, she determined to nip her feelings in the bud.

"What are you thinking?" Barrett leaned his hip on the side of the counter. "Looks like you are deep in thought about now. Probably wondering about what just happened."

"Hey, that's none of my business." She waved both hands in front of her chest. "I just work here."

"I think you and I both know better than that." He held her gaze until she broke eye contact.

Her stomach flip-flopped worse than that time she ate some bad tuna fish. "I don't know."

"We need to talk." He lowered his voice. "About what you overheard at Sam's."

"I agree." She met his gaze. "If I had known you and her were having a private conversation, I would never have come inside."

"That's on me, not you. Tell me how you found the jump drive again."

After she filled him in on the room cleaning situation, he nodded. "Can you meet me behind Whale's Tail at seven?"

"What for?" She dropped her hands behind the counter, fidgeting with her fingers.

"It's private, so we can discuss things." He gave her a knowing look.

"Oh, yes. That makes sense." She gulped a mouthful of air. "I can be there."

Even though dusk had fallen, Lottie drove by Whale's Tail three times before she found a parking spot. With the beach being the main attraction, people could park on the roadside or walk down the street. Lottie had no intention of leaving her car far away in case she needed to leave quickly. Not that she didn't trust Barrett. But she didn't *fully* trust him.

Barrett stood and waved, his loose white button-up flowing around him as the wind kicked up. Her brown Birkenstock sandals sunk into the warm white sand as she padded toward the picnic table farthest from the rest. The sandals had been a Christmas gift from Frankie and Alex. She was thankful she'd changed into blue jean shorts and a turquoise blue shirt before she left the bed and breakfast. Otherwise, she would've looked like a frumpy alley cat who ate fifteen too many mice compared to Barrett, the expensive, gorgeous cat who ate the finest foods from Taylor Swift's table.

"Thank you for coming." He motioned for her to sit.

As she lowered herself at the picnic table, a sense of dread nearly caused her to pass out. "It's not a problem." She said as she took inventory of the area.

After the waiter took their orders, Barrett leaned both elbows on the picnic table. "I'm following my gut on this one. Since you saved my nephew's life, I will break the rules and tell you what I can."

"I also already know. Remember, I heard you say what you are."

"True. I guess it's out of my hands."

"Yep."

"I'm a retired marine. Some people think I have a bad attitude and a problem with authority." He shrugged.

"Hmm, I wonder why."

He raised a brow but kept going with his story. "Over the past year, there's been an uptick in home invasions along the coast among other things."

"I've heard about that. Too bad they haven't caught the people yet."

"The thing is, it's never the same people. The victims' descriptions are always very different."

"So, several people are doing the same thing?"

"That, or we have one person in charge of a group." He raised his index finger, signaling Lottie to be quiet.

With a smile, the waiter placed two platters of fish tacos on the picnic table. "Let me know if I can get you anything else." He said with a thick Russian accent before greeting a group of people who claimed the picnic table next to theirs.

"Could it be –"

Barrett shook his head and glanced at the group of people. "Let's change the subject."

"I have more to say. Things I need to share about my past."

"Let's meet again tomorrow night." He cocked his head. "I'll take you out on my boat."

"As long as you don't plan on dumping me in the ocean." She bit her lip before a bark of laughter escaped.

"Ha, you have jokes. I like that."

She shrugged. "Yeah, I can be funny on occasion."

"There's more to you than meets the eye, Lottie McKenna."

To keep from freaking out and making a fool of herself, she focused on her plate. She squirted lime on a taco, added a scoop of slaw, and took a bite. As the sweet yet spicy flavors mingled in her mouth, she promised herself she'd be back at Whale's Tail.

A grin lit Barrett's face. "Good, huh?"

"Delicious."

He grasped her hand in his. "Thank you."

She bobbed her head as zings went straight from where his hand held hers to her heart. As she pulled her hand away, she knew without a doubt that this man was everything she'd ever dreamed of.

Too bad he could never be hers.

Chapter 21

Family First Auto took up half a block on Mira-cle Strip Parkway. Lottie's brow raised as she peered through the floor-to-ceiling windows. Frosty and a younger man stood by a black Mustang with purple trim. They seemed to be in deep conversation.

She made her way inside, her sights set on Frosty.

A stunning woman with rich, dark skin greeted her with a warm smile. "Good afternoon, and wel-come to Family First Auto," she said, her excited energy contagious.

"Good afternoon," Lottie replied with a smile of her own.

Frosty spun around, his face lighting up like a child with a new favorite toy when he met Lottie's gaze. "What a pleasant surprise," he exclaimed as he strode toward them. "Are you in the market for a new car?"

Lottie shook her head, a half-smile playing on her lips. "No, I haven't had my current car for very long. I was thinking about your offer and decided to come by and check out the place."

With a gentle touch, he rested his hand on her elbow, his eyes conveying enthusiasm. "Then why don't we move into my office for a chat? It'll be more comfortable there."

"All right," she agreed, doing her best to hide her nervousness at the prospect of their conversation as they stepped away from the bustle of the showroom.

Once inside the basic car dealer office, Lottie sat in one of two brown leather chairs as Frosty poured two cups of black coffee. He sat one in front of Lottie. "Tell me what you've been up to these past twenty years."

"I promise you don't have the time, or if I remember correctly, the patience to sit for that long." Lottie smiled a genuine smile. There had been a time when Frosty had treated Lottie with kindness. And how could she regret her past that led her to meet Eddie because without him there would be no Rhnae.

He laughed and slapped the desk. "You have a good memory. So, do you have any sales experience?"

"Not really sales, but I've worked at a hotel and now the bed and breakfast."

"Okay okay. When do you want to go to work?"

"Well, I need to get through this rehab, so I'd need at least a few months."

"I can respect that." He rubbed his goatee and stared at her face. "You look good, Lottie. Really."

Her cheeks heated with the compliment. "Thank you, Frosty."

He gestured around the office. "Can you believe I'm a legitimate businessman now?"

"That's unexpected, but I'm thrilled for you."

"How's your family doing?"

"Honestly? My daughter holds my past against me."

"Daughter, huh? Other than that, you're all by yourself?"

Someone pecked on the door. Lottie turned and met Coco's dark gaze. Her heart sped into high drive when he stepped inside. The slacks, yellow button-up, and suit jacket were far from the saggy jeans and tank top he wore at the hotel. His eyes darted from her to Frosty.

Frosty stood. "Look who we have here. Lottie McKenna in the flesh."

Lottie found her feet and hugged Coco. "Good to see you, Coco."

"You, too." He removed a pen he had stuck behind his ear and flipped it around in his hand. "Boss, we have a customer who wants a deal on that 2014 Audi."

With a grin, he glanced at Lottie. "Please excuse me."

As soon as the door shut behind Frosty, Coco grabbed the chair beside her. "Have you told Frosty about the other night?"

"I haven't said a word," she replied, her voice steady despite the tension in the air.

He released a shaky breath, relief washing over his face. "Oh, thank the Lord," he murmured, rubbing the back of his neck as if trying to ease an invisible weight.

She shifted her gaze, studying him closely. "So, I take it he doesn't know about your... um, side job?"

His eyes widened slightly, and he leaned in closer, his voice dropping to a whisper. "Please don't say anything. This must stay between us."

"I won't say a word," she assured him, her tone serious. "But if he's not the boss, then who is?"

He hesitated for a moment, glancing around as if checking for eavesdroppers before finally speaking. "Let's just say there's someone we both should avoid getting on the wrong side of." His expression darkened, causing a shiver to run down Lottie's spine.

Lottie furrowed her brow. "What exactly are they in charge of? I'm not quite following."

Coco bit his fingernails, a nervous habit he had even when they were teenagers. "Honestly, you don't need to worry about that," he replied. "But tell me, are you and Barrett Donahue an item, or what's going on there?"

"Not at all. We've only just met," Lottie replied, striving to maintain a casual tone despite the implications of his question.

"Just met? Then what were you doing with him at a hotel?" He leaned in, eyebrows raised, as if searching for answers.

Lottie took a deep breath, willing herself to remain calm. "Well, when I say we just met, I meant I know his sister, so it's not completely out of the blue."

His expression twisted into a frown. "Has he confided in you about anything?"

"Confided? About what exactly? I work for him, so he's shared quite a bit regarding hotel operations and management with me," she replied, smiling gently, hoping to put Coco at ease.

"I guess you still find bad boys attractive?"

Frosty opened the door, a smile covering his face. "Go on out there and work that deal, Coco. They're buying the Audi."

Coco fist-bumped Frosty on the way out.

Lottie released the breath she'd been holding. What a weird situation. Who was the criminal...Frosty or Coco? Or were they both?

Whoever it was, Lottie had no intention of getting involved.

Chapter 22

Waves hissed against the docks as Barrett approached his 2014 Sunseeker San Remo Motor Yacht. It had been his pride and joy since he'd first stepped foot in it after leaving the Marines four years ago. The sleek vessel was designed with a striking two-tone color scheme: the top was a pristine white, while the bottom gleamed in a glossy black finish, making it reminiscent of a cutting-edge, futuristic boat. He stole a glance at Lottie, unsure why her opinion mattered so much.

"Wow," she exclaimed, her voice filled with excitement as she descended the four steps into the boat's interior behind him.

As he surveyed the space, memories flooded back of the awe he'd felt when he first decided to purchase it. The main area had a spacious and inviting layout, featuring a contemporary dining table surrounded by soft white leather seating wrapped around three sides. The warm tones of the furniture contrasted beautifully with the sleek design of the kitchenette, which was equipped with modern appliances and polished surfaces. Nearby, a flat-screen television hung on the wall, completing the cozy yet sophisticated atmosphere of the living space.

"I hope you're hungry," he said as a strange and unwelcome flopping kicked up in his belly.

Lottie's lashes flew high, and she nodded. "Whatever you had brought in smells too good to say no to."

"Brought in?" He bit his lip and debated telling Lottie he had cooked the meal. She already seemed nervous, so he had better keep that information to himself. "Lobster Fettucine Alfredo, garlic bread, and a side salad."

He sounded like an idiot. Why had he made such an elaborate meal? Lottie probably thought he was interested in dating her. That or desperate.

Luckily, the conversation flowed smoothly as they ate and made small talk. She wiped her mouth with a napkin and laid it on her lap. "After our parents were killed, my sister Helen and I ended up at the Children's Home in Pensacola. I met Coco a few months later."

She sipped her sparkling water and took a deep breath. "Helen hit it off with Larry Kingston, and I let jealousy eat me up. So, I started hanging out with Coco more and more until we plotted our escape and ran away."

Barrett paused, swallowing a bite of salad. A wave of sympathy washed over him for the younger Lottie. "I'm truly sorry about what happened to your parents," he said softly, his voice laced with genuine concern.

"Thank you," she said, a hint of sadness creeping into her voice. "We ended up in Alabama, staying with Coco's friend, Frosty Corbitt. I thought he was kind for taking a couple of teenage runaways in, but it didn't take long for things to spiral." A bitter laugh rose from her chest, and her eyes glistened with unshed tears. "Frosty ended up putting me to work running drugs. It was a harsh reality I wasn't prepared for."

Barrett looked at her intently. "Lottie, you don't have to share this if it's too painful."

"I decided to leave Alabama after discovering that Frosty was planning to kick me out. His new girlfriend had taken an instant dislike to me, which made things unbearable for both of us."

"And where did you end up going?"

"I met Eddie Chambers at a New Year's Eve party in 1999. We hit it off, and I felt a spark of hope for a fresh start. By the end of the night, I decided to leave for Miami with him. Eddie's family owned a grocery store chain there, and he offered me a job. It felt like the opportunity I needed."

"Have you seen Frosty or Coco since?"

"Not until this past week. I want you to know I am not involved in anything they're doing." She shared details of her meeting with Frosty at the bed and breakfast and then her visit to the car dealership.

He tapped his chin and met Lottie's gaze as he absorbed her words, fully convinced of her sincerity. "That is interesting. I can't imagine Coco in a suit."

Lottie sighed and shook her head. "I don't want to get entangled in any of this. My main focus is to get my life back on track and return home to my daughter."

He raised an eyebrow. It's a good thing he decided not to say anything about his upcoming meeting with Coco. "Daughter? How old is she?"

With a smile, Lottie reached for her phone and scrolled. She turned the screen toward him, revealing a photo of a pretty dark-haired girl posing gleefully on the beach.

As he examined the picture, a smile spread across his face. "She's a cute kid, Lottie," he said, waiting for her to question his situation like most women. How many kids do you have? Are you married? Ever been married? Want to be married?

Instead, she put away her phone and took another bite of pasta, washing it down with sparkling water. "Have you had a chance to see what's on that jump drive I found?"

"No, I haven't had the chance." Now that Lottie hadn't asked the questions, he wanted to know why. Did she not find him attractive? His eyes gaped, and he swallowed. Now was not the time to develop feelings for Lottie McKenna. Not only would he rather not be tied to anyone, but he also had the feeling that Lottie would not welcome his advances. Which was fine by him.

Marriage wouldn't be a mistake he'd make. Alyssa breaking off their engagement and leaving the rehab two years ago had saved him from many heartaches.

Once back at the bed and breakfast, Lottie escaped upstairs, and Barrett beelined to his office. With a swift motion, he retrieved the jump drive from his desk drawer and inserted it into the USB port of his desktop computer.

The buzzing whir of the computer filled the air, and a spreadsheet of sales transactions for home goods filled the screen. As he leaned in closer, he figured one of their weekend guests had inadvertently left the jump drive behind. He scrolled down the sheet, seeking names to help him reunite the jump drive with its rightful owner. However, as his eyes scanned the columns, he found no names, no identifying details to connect any person to the jump drive.

Just as he was about to give up, a thought occurred, and he right-clicked and selected unhide. In an instant, a second page materialized, exposing a list of home addresses from Perdido Key to Panama City Beach. Odd. The whimsical pink hearts next to several addresses aroused his curiosity even more. Not only that, but the addresses seemed familiar.

He sucked in a sharp breath as he unlocked a wall safe hidden behind a false panel. A stack of police reports lay stacked neatly inside. As he thumbed through them, each address with reported home invasions matched the houses marked with hearts on the spreadsheet.

After closing the safe, he sank into his office chair. A memory surfaced from when he was engaged to Alyssa. She had created a to-do list for their engagement party, and each time she completed a task, she marked it off with a heart.

Chapter 23

Comfortable in loose jeans and a Pensacola Beach t-shirt, Lottie took a bite of scrambled eggs and washed it down with coffee. She glanced at the flyer on the table and sighed. Keatyn Griffin, the preacher's wife from Pensacola, was scheduled to speak at Oak Grove church of Christ today.

Frankie had called the night before to let her know she would be there. Rhnae had flown back to Arkansas with Simon and Vandon for the week. Lottie was happy Rhnae could get out and do the things she never could as a teenager.

Even though both Samantha and Frankie invited Lottie, she hesitated to go. Didn't people dress up for ladies' day events? Lottie would be out of place in her casual clothes. She picked up her phone and looked at the picture of Rhnae she kept as her screensaver.

Alyssa Blankenship whirled into the room and grabbed a cinnamon roll. She glanced at Lottie's phone before meeting her gaze. "Have you seen Barrett this morning?"

"I haven't," Lottie replied with a smile instead of getting up and dumping her coffee on Alyssa's head. She locked her phone and swallowed, embarrassed by her mean-spirited thoughts. "I'm sure he's around here somewhere."

Before Alyssa answered, Samantha poked her head inside the breakfast area. She ignored Alyssa and looked at Lottie. "Are you ready to go?"

Oh no. She'd forgotten all about telling Samantha she'd go with her. Now what? Take ill?

"Um, I don't really feel like going."

Samantha stepped inside, her hand flying to the hip of her designer jeans. "Come on."

"Where are you trying to make her go?" Alyssa butted into the conversation.

Lottie handed Alyssa the flyer. "To a ladies' day."

"You can't force your employees to go places with you, Samantha." Alyssa's tone oozed smugness.

With a sweet smile, Samantha replied, "You really should consider joining us."

"I don't think so," Alyssa stated firmly, waving a dismissive hand as she turned to leave. Glancing back at Lottie, she added, "Just remember, you don't have to do what she says on your day off."

"It's not like that," Lottie said, feeling the need to defend Samantha. She then turned to Samantha, her expression brightening. "I'm actually happy to go. Should I change into something else first?"

Samantha shook her head with a reassuring smile. "You look great just the way you are."

An hour later, Lottie introduced Samantha to her niece, Frankie Foster, and the speaker, Keatyn Griffin. After warm greetings, the group settled into their seats in the third row, ready to enjoy the event together.

After one of the ladies graciously introduced Keatyn, she beamed at the audience, her smile warm and inviting as she expressed her gratitude for the opportunity to speak. Her captivating turquoise blue eyes shimmered like jewels, catching the light in a way that accentuated the delicate features of her face.

"I remember not being great at taking instructions when I was younger. I often only heard what I wanted to hear. One day, I learned an important lesson about listening. My brother, Alvin, got his car stuck in our backyard. He asked me to hit the gas while he pushed. It seemed simple enough."

She smiled like she was reliving the memory as she spoke. "I heard him tell me to put the car in reverse and hit the gas, but I must have tuned out after that. I pressed the gas pedal so hard that the car flew backward, across the highway, and landed in a ditch."

Laughter echoed across the auditorium. "Brake! BRAKE! I heard Alvin screaming with his hands flailing in the air."

Keatyn paused and shook her head. "After the car stopped, I was shaken up, and so was Alvin. He was possibly a little mad but couldn't stay mad for long. See, I was the big sister. You probably thought Alvin was older, but that's not the case. Let's just say I was a little preoccupied with myself as a teenager."

"It took me until my thirties to realize that my experience with my brother taught me a valuable lesson. I should have listened to everything Alvin said before getting behind the wheel. Just as that car situation could have had serious consequences, the situations we find ourselves in as adults can have eternal consequences. We must recognize that our choices can lead to lasting impacts."

"If I had died or harmed someone, it would have been a tragedy. How much worse will it be for those who ignore God's commands? Refusing to listen leads to sin, which results in eternal death."

"Living with the guilt of my death would have been difficult for Alvin to bear, and thankfully, he didn't have to. Memories can bring both happiness and pain. Have you considered how you'll cope with the memories of your actions and inactions in life? Our memories will follow us. Those who refuse to obey God will remember every opportunity they had to change their lives and the loved ones who tried to guide them. The last chance they had to obey Christ will replay in their minds, a haunting reminder of what could have been."

Lottie squirmed, unease tearing through her stomach.

"We have an example of how our memories follow us with the account of the rich man and Lazarus in Luke 16. The rich man remembered his life even after he went to torment."

Keatyn delicately turned the pages of her Bible, the faint rustle of paper contrasting with the heavy silence that hung in the air. Her lips curled downward with a sadness Lottie understood too well. "I can't imagine the pain those memories caused him. He suffered torment and lived with the regret of not obeying God when he had the chance. I was lucky to land safely in a ditch across the highway. As you think about where your life will end, consider this: Are you taking steps to ensure you go to Heaven? Are you seeking God's will through Bible study and understanding His requirements? Reflect on these questions and act if needed. Put God first, aim for Heaven, and begin your journey today."

After a potluck lunch, Lottie climbed into the plush interior of Samantha's gleaming brown Mercedes GLC300. She settled into the buttery seat, her gaze drifting out of the window as the landscape of houses and palm trees blurred by. Samantha drove in silence, seemingly caught up in her thoughts.

A flutter of anxiety danced in Lottie's stomach as she considered putting God first. Was she taking steps to get to Heaven? Or had her life been made up of pity parties? What if she put God and others first? How might such a shift reshape her life, especially her relationship with Rhnae? She needed to change.

Her heart picked up its pace as she determined how to do it. Since she had a relationship with Frosty and Coco, she would dive into Barrett's investigation and help him figure out what was happening.

It shouldn't be too dangerous. Right?

Chapter 24

After her morning shift and session with Samantha, Lottie tucked the latest John Grisham book under her arm and headed to the gazebo behind the bed and breakfast. She set her phone, the book, and a glass of iced tea on the table.

She picked her phone up and texted Rhnae.

> *How are you enjoying your last summer before you're a senior?*

> *Good! Vandon asked if I can go with her & Simon to NYC*

> *Do you want to go?*

> *I do!*

What does Frankie and Alex think?

They want your opinion.

I think you should go and have fun!

Okay!

I'll cash app you some spending money!

Thank you, Mama!

You're welcome. I sure love you!

I love you!

I'm glad you're getting help.

Lottie loved the message and smiled as she laid her phone down. Things were going to work out with Rhnae—she just knew it. Once she finished rehab, Lottie planned to have an open, honest conversation about their past. But first, Lottie needed to forgive herself.

"Isn't your name Lottie?" Alyssa Blankenship asked as she sauntered around the gazebo. Her glimmering black glittery booty shorts caught the sunlight, drawing attention to her confident stride, and her tank top highlighted her toned arms.

"Yes, that's me. Can I help you with something?" Lottie replied, trying to gauge the intent behind Alyssa's cheerful demeanor.

"Possibly. I'm curious about something. Do you enjoy working here?" Alyssa inquired, her tone light yet probing as she leaned against one of the gazebo's wooden supports.

"It's good overall. I like the atmosphere and the people." Lottie wiped the moisture around her glass with a napkin before meeting Alyssa's gaze. "Why do you ask?"

"Well, how would you feel about making some extra cash?" Alyssa's eyes sparkled with excitement as if she were sharing a secret.

"That depends on what you have in mind," Lottie replied with a brow raised.

"Are you opposed to getting your hands dirty?" Alyssa stared at Lottie intently.

"What do you mean by that?"

"We can talk more about it later," Alyssa said, her voice dropping to a conspiratorial whisper as she began to walk away. But as she turned to leave, she stopped, glancing back at Lottie. "By the way, I really dislike how Samantha pressured you into attending that event the other day."

"Oh, she didn't," Lottie clarified, shaking her head.

"I admire your loyalty and how you stand by your employer."

Lottie's cheeks heated. "I didn't really do anything special."

"Well, I still think you're a loyal employee. I appreciate that since I have every intention of marrying Barrett."

Lottie's eyes narrowed, disbelief flickering across her face. "Really?"

"Yes, I'm so lucky to have another chance with him."

"That's...nice." Lottie attempted to mask her disappointment by running a hand through her hair.

"He's making me dinner tonight," Alyssa continued. "He's such a wonderful cook, and I can't wait for our perfect makeup meal."

Lottie snatched the book and stood. "I hope you enjoy it."

Alyssa's face lit up with a bright smile. "I'm serious about you working for me. It'll be an easy way to make some extra cash."

Lottie watched Alyssa gracefully move around the side of the bed and breakfast, taking in the swaying palm trees and cheerful ambiance. The fabric of the back window curtains fluttered slightly. Lottie caught the eye of Mildred in the window. The moment their gazes met, Mildred quickly closed the blinds. The poor woman seemed painfully bored, waiting for her back to heal. She kept showing up where Lottie was. If Lottie was still a paranoid person, she'd swear Mildred was spying on her.

With a sigh, Lottie cut off her silly thoughts, opened her book, and scanned the first paragraph of chapter one. However, the words quickly blurred together in her mind. The thought of Barrett and

Alyssa heading out on a date made it impossible for her to focus.

A heavy weight pressed down on her heart, a familiar ache accompanying her struggle to accept the painful truth that someone like Barrett would never look twice at a nobody like her. The image of Alyssa flitting around him, her charm and vibrant energy radiating like sunlight, made Lottie's stomach churn.

In her last session with her counselor, they discussed Lottie's path to accepting and loving herself. She'd reminded Lottie to recognize her past while celebrating who she is today. They discussed how those past mistakes do not determine her value. Why should they? She's not the same person she was back then.

There's no reason Barrett wouldn't give her a chance.

The question was, would Lottie give herself a chance?

Chapter 25

The twenty-minute ride to Fort Walton Beach had Barrett questioning his sanity for making reservations at Old Bay Steamer. Not the ride itself but Alyssa's nonstop chattering about everything she wanted in life. Things summed it up.

He glanced at her from the corner of his eye. Yes, she had outward beauty with her exotic green eyes and long red curls flowing past her slim shoulders. But that was it.

"I still can't believe you're not cooking for me, Barrett." Alyssa's lips turned downward as her words came out in a whine.

"Yeah, I know. I would've if it hadn't been for Samantha." He slowed his Camaro down at the red light in front of Alvin's Island, doing his best to sound as disappointed as Alyssa expected him to be.

"What did she do?" Her forehead creased. Samantha had never liked Alyssa, and the feeling had been mutual.

"My session went longer than it should have," he said as he pulled into the only empty parking spot. Thank goodness he'd made a reservation. "She didn't know I was meeting you."

"What were you doing then?"

He lowered his head as if in shame. "Look, Alyssa, there's some things about me you don't know. Honestly, I don't want you to."

"What kind of things?" She pinned him with her gaze.

"If I tell you, I imagine this relationship will be over before it can begin again." He nearly grimaced. Hopefully he wasn't laying it on too thick. "Your daddy would never allow…"

"Allow what?" She leaned closer, her voice a mere whisper.

"You to get involved with someone like me. I'm not the same man you knew. A lot happened in my life after losing you."

"Tell me."

Her interest seemed so genuine he almost felt bad for leading her on like this. But if his instincts were right, lives were at stake and Alyssa was involved. "I turned to drugs after you left me. It didn't last long, but now Samantha guilts me into attending counseling with her."

"Is that all? I'm okay with that."

"No, that's not all." He sighed and rubbed his hand on the back of his neck. "Uncle Elliott owns the majority of the bed and breakfast." He stared ahead for a second. "I'm living in one of the suites because I don't have the funds for my own place right now."

"So, you're struggling financially?" She sounded more pleased than she should have, considering the circumstances.

"I've had to make some tough decisions, and I don't think you should be getting involved with me."

She gripped his hand in hers. "Let me decide for myself."

"There's no way your daddy will let you get back together with... a person like me."

"You let me deal with Daddy." She grinned. "Tell me, are you involved with the lady working for you?"

"Who?"

"What's her name...Lucy?" She tapped her chin. "No, her name is Lottie."

"Oh, her?" He grimaced. "Samantha hired her without even asking me. I think she's there to make a little money and then leave."

"What makes you say that?"

"I've seen a lot of people like her over the years. The type who work a job for a few weeks only to get money to support their habit, then they disappear."

"So you think she's just there for a paycheck?"

"Until you asked, I haven't given it much thought. She's doing a necessary job. After that, what she does is none of my business."

"What would you say if I could get you a job where you'd never have to answer to your uncle again?"

"I'd say that's too good to be true."

"Not necessarily. Why did you say I shouldn't get involved with you? Are you doing something illegal?"

"I don't want to get you involved. Okay? Please let's just have dinner for old times sake then you go find an upstanding, morally solid man."

She laughed before leaning close, pecking his lips. "There are some things you need to know, and I promise to tell you. Soon."

As the hostess welcomed them with a warm smile, the irresistible aroma of perfectly seasoned lobster and shrimp, rich with garlic and herbs, filled the air. The tantalizing scent drew Barrett further into the bustling atmosphere filled with laughter and clinking glasses. He returned the hostess's smile, a flicker of satisfaction lighting up his face, knowing he was closer than ever to unraveling the mystery. Who would've imagined that the key to the intricate puzzle would lead back to his ex-girlfriend? Not him, but deep down, his instincts screamed that Alyssa Blankenship was deeply entangled in criminal activity.

As the night continued over a delicious meal, it became clearer that her involvement ran far deeper than mere coincidence. Barrett hated it, but he would have to get close to her again to uncover the truth behind her calculated facade.

<h1 style="text-align:center">Chapter 26</h1>

THEN: 2018

Until today, Lottie had never considered how it felt to be dragged behind a vehicle on a gravel road. Blood dripped from her mouth and nose as she scurried into the bathroom. A wave of relief hit when water spurted out of the faucet. She carefully dabbed at her face with a wet washrag.

"Where did you go?" Eddie stomped through the bedroom, the old wooden floor creaking with each step.

Her heart tripled in speed. "I'm just trying to wash my face a little."

He snaked his hand out and grabbed the back of her neck, pulling downward until she nearly fell to her knees. "I wasn't done talking to you, woman."

After dragging her into the kitchen, he shoved her onto one of the wooden chairs that had meant so much to her. Her gaze moved around the room, landing on a sledgehammer that leaned against the cabinet. "I'm done with this. You broke my chair. So what? I don't care. It's just a chair."

"That's not what you said earlier. Remember? You screamed at me over a chair." He picked up the sledgehammer and slammed it into the other two chairs before moving to the table. Each whack intensified the pounding that coursed through her head. When the table and chairs lay in a heap under the window, he turned to Lottie. "You will never, and I mean ever, raise your voice at me again. If you do, you'll get the same treatment as your precious table and chairs."

Her stomach churned as he moved closer. "I won't, Eddie," she whispered, her eyes meeting his.

"You keep the chair you're sitting in as a reminder of what could happen to you."

She lowered her eyes, waiting for the next blow. Instead, he picked her up by her throat and slammed her into the wall.

The front door opened, and Rhnae ran inside. "Daddy, get off my Mama!" She said, tugging at his pants.

Eddie backhanded Rhnae, causing her to tumble onto the wooden pieces, where she began to cry.

A surge of heat enveloped Lottie, giving her strength. She shoved Eddie away and fell to the floor beside Rhnae, scooping her into a hug. "It's okay, baby girl."

"Looks like you both need to be taught a lesson." Eddie's voice lowered, and Lottie sensed a shift in his demeanor. In all her ten years, Eddie had never hit Rhnae. Now that it had happened, what would stop him from going farther?

Lottie wrapped a shaky hand around a jagged leg from one of the chairs. She would not let him lay another finger on Rhnae. She leaned into Rhnae's ear and whispered, "Run as fast as you can to the grocery store down the road and hide in their bathroom."

Eddie watched Rhnae leave before turning bloodshot eyes to Lottie. "That's probably best."

Lottie prayed for strength as she stood.

Laughter roared from Eddie as he laid his eyes on the makeshift weapon in Lottie's hand. "You really are stupid, ain't you?"

She raised her hand high. "Stay back."

The door opened, and Eddie's latest side woman stepped inside. "I thought we were going out tonight." Her eyes widened as she backed out the door. "Sorry. I didn't realize."

"Wait for me in the car. I'm coming." As the door clicked shut, Eddie kissed Lottie on the cheek. "I'll be back soon, darling."

"No rush."

He kissed her lips before running his hand down her face. She winced as he dug his fingers into the bruises. "I look forward to our next talk. I left you a little something to make you feel better in the bathroom cabinet."

For the first time in years, Lottie held Eddie's gaze. "I got plans to change my ways and do better."

He barked a laugh. "You will never be anything but trash. I'm the only man who will ever love you." His gaze moved to the broken pieces of wood. "This better be cleaned up when I get home."

As soon as Eddie and his girlfriend drove away, Lottie bolted into action. She locked the front door, ran to her closet, and moved the broken ceiling tile away, pulling out her stash of money. Pushing past the pain that screamed for her to stop, she grabbed an overnight bag and threw a few outfits and essentials in it for her and Rhnae. She paused outside the bathroom door, blew out her breath, and snatched the plastic baggie from the cabinet. As she stuffed it in her pocket with a mental promise, she was only taking it in case she needed money.

Her gaze landed on the single chair left standing as she headed to the door. With a guttural cry, she picked up the sledgehammer and beat the chair until it collapsed onto the floor. She didn't need a reminder of this life. Eddie could have it.

Robin, her friend who worked at the tiny one-room grocery store, gasped when Lottie walked inside. "Oh no, Lottie. What happened?"

"It's a long story." Lottie grasped Robin's hands. "Thank you for everything you've done for me, especially Rhnae."

Robin's eyes widened. "Are you finally leaving?"

Lottie nodded. "I need to buy a few essentials, and then we're gone. The only thing I'll miss about this place is you."

"I'll miss you both," Robin said as she handed Lottie a wad of bills.

"I can't take your money." Lottie shook her head.

"I've been saving it for you. Now go and make yourself a new life for you and your baby girl."

As Lottie drove into Tampa a few hours later, she prayed she would find the strength to do what Robin said. If only making a new life was as easy as it sounded.

Chapter 27

Present Day

The latest session with her counselor had lifted Lottie's spirits so much that she went straight to see Samantha afterward. As she left Samantha's office, she couldn't help but smile.

"That smile looks good on you." Barrett crossed his arms and leaned against the empty secretary's desk. "I hope my session goes so well."

Lottie wrapped both hands around her throat to mask the heat running up her neck. "I hope so, too."

As she attempted to shuffle past Barrett, he blocked her. "Will you have a seat?" Without waiting for an answer, he led her to the soft orange leather sofa. He shifted his body to face her. "Tell me something, have you interacted much with Alyssa Blankenship since she's been at the bed and breakfast?"

She crossed her legs and met his gaze. "A little."

His lashes beat softly, but he didn't break the connection between their eyes. After a very long two or three seconds, he finally spoke. "She grilled me about you."

"She offered me a job yesterday." Lottie kept her eyes glued to Barrett's, curious about his reaction.

That seemed to pique his interest. He leaned forward. "What kind of job?"

"I'm not sure. She said it would be easy money but refused to give me details." Lottie's brow furrowed as she recalled the weird conversation.

Barrett tapped his chin, his eyes narrowing. "That's quite unusual. Alyssa doesn't work."

"Oh, she also raved about how good of a cook you are." Lottie scooted close to the arm of the sofa. "Did she enjoy the dinner you made her last night?"

"I took her to Old Bay Steamer since I'm trying to win her over for information." A playful grin crossed his face as he regarded her with amusement. "If I didn't know any better, I might think you're jealous."

She laced her arms over her chest as her jaw hung open. "I most certainly am not jealous."

"Okay," he replied with a raised brow.

"Alyssa did ask me if I was opposed to getting my hands dirty." Lottie cocked her head, changing the subject. "What do you think she meant by that?"

"Nothing good." He anchored his gaze to hers. "I know you said you don't want to get involved, but you may already be. Now is the time to decide whether you want to stay out of this."

"What do you mean?"

"I believe Alyssa may be involved with Frosty and Coco. I also know you have an in with all three that could be helpful."

"I want to help." She contained the moisture pushing against her eyelids.

"Coco says they have a job for me that won't be easy. I should know more soon."

"Let me know what I can do to help. This is the first time I've had a chance to make a real difference, so count me in."

"All right. I'll talk to my commissioner to see if we can bring you in."

"Sounds great. I'm heading to Pensacola to pick up some clothes and things. Maybe we can meet up this evening?"

"Lottie McKenna, are you asking me on a date?"

Barrett's playful tone warmed her insides and her cheeks. Why was she acting like a schoolgirl with a crush? Before she could answer, Samantha poked her head out the door. She smiled knowingly at Barrett and Lottie before glancing at her watch. "I have another appointment in thirty minutes."

"I'm coming. I'm coming."

As Lottie backed out of her parking spot, she couldn't help but wonder why Barrett still had sessions with Samantha. It's not like he was a drug addict. Maybe it was part of his cover. She shrugged and daydreamed of her reunion with Rhnae as she passed a Chevrolet Traverse.

By the time Lottie drove into Pensacola, the sun had dipped low on the horizon, leaving behind a dusky hue that bathed the streets in soft, muted colors. After finding a spot to park along the tree-lined street, she took a moment to gaze at Frankie's charming historic home that had once belonged to Frankie's grandparents. The warm lights from inside illuminated the windows. Inside, Frankie and her husband, Alex, were seated at the dinner table, caught up in a lively card game, their faces full of laughter.

Suddenly, a flood of bittersweet memories surged within her. She was transported back a few years, standing in the very same spot where she had watched her late sister, Helen, and her husband, Larry, sharing laughter and stories at that same table. The image of their warmth and joy contrasted sharply with her regret.

Lottie's heart ached as she thought about how she would give almost anything to return to that night—to have a conversation, express her love, and bridge the distance between them. If only she hadn't let envy and pride dictate her actions. Those feelings ultimately led her to miss her last opportunity to connect with her sister before it was too late. The weight of that missed chance hung heavily on her, a haunting reminder of how vital it is to cherish every moment with loved ones. She promised herself that she would be better and do better for Rhnae, Frankie, and their loved ones. Barrett's face floated through her mind as she walked up the steps to the front door.

Chapter 28

Barrett strode toward Samantha's cluttered desk, a mix of determination and uncertainty swirling within him. He sank into the leather chair and gazed forlornly out the door, where he and Lottie had stood only moments before, the remnants of their conversation lingering in his mind. He bit his lip, struggling with the strange feeling that had taken hold of him—how had he let her affect him so much? He had promised himself not to get involved with her, particularly given the gravity of the case weighing heavily on his shoulders.

"Are you interested in Lottie?" Samantha asked, her sharp gaze cutting through his act. It was almost eerie how well she could see through his emotions.

He waved a dismissive hand, attempting to brush off the implication. "Not at all."

Samantha rested her chin thoughtfully on her hand, then leaned forward, her elbow propped on the desk as if bracing herself for a deeper conversation. "I think you're lying to either me or yourself," she replied, an insightful smirk creeping onto her lips.

"It doesn't matter," he insisted, shaking his head with a hint of irritation. "I have to focus on this case right now."

"I understand," she said, her expression softening. "Lottie is a nice woman with a troubled past, but I genuinely believe she wants to become the person God intended her to be."

He cut his eyes at Samantha, weary that she would bring God up again. It's not that he had anything against God. Not really. He just didn't want to be a hypocrite. "That's nice for her, but listen, I know you have an appointment coming up, so let's move on," he urged, hoping to divert the conversation.

"Fine," Samantha said, her eyes narrowing with curiosity. "What have you found out? Is Alyssa involved in what's been happening?"

"It looks that way." Barrett's tone was grave as he recounted the details of their tense dinner and the cryptic call from Coco.

"I think you're right," she said, her brow furrowed with concern.

His phone buzzed with an incoming text.

Meet me at Bass Pro. 7 pm

See you then

He laid his phone down. "That's Coco. We're meeting at 7 tonight."

"Maybe you'll finally get some real info."

"Yes. Just so you know, I'm bringing Lottie in," Barrett declared, an edge of resolution creeping into his voice.

"What? Why would you do that?" Her eyes widened and her tone sharpened.

"Alyssa has recruited her, and she knows Coco. Lottie might be able to get valuable information to help unravel this mess."

"Okay," Samantha said slowly, nodding in agreement. "Whatever it takes to bring our cousin's killer to justice. But keep Lottie safe. I like her."

Right on time, Barrett moseyed around Bass Pro in Destin, stopping at the fishing gear. What he'd give to be here shopping for a deep-sea fishing trip. But that wasn't the case. After retiring from the Marines, life had been far from the peaceful beach lifestyle he'd envisioned.

Coco appeared beside him, picking up a tackle box. Barrett took a second look at him. In his straight-legged jeans and deep purple button-up shirt, he almost didn't recognize him. Coco grinned. "What do you think? Is this a good brand?"

"I think so."

"Your job is to break into a safe and bring me the contents by the end of the day tomorrow."

"Why me?"

"You'll see," Coco replied and remained quiet for a moment, his attention on reading a bait package. "What's your opinion on that fishing boat?" Coco's gaze moved to the smaller of three boats displayed in the showroom.

"It's nice. I like how it's not too big, but appears large enough for a good time at sea."

Coco nodded. "I especially like the tires. You should check them out." With that, he turned and headed in the other direction.

Barrett eyeballed a few more items on the shelf, picked up the tackle box Coco admired, and headed toward the boat. He glanced around the area. Most shoppers seemed lost in their thoughts and uninterested in what Barrett was doing. He felt around the tires and found nothing until the back left one. He kept the small envelope in his hand as he appraised the boat.

A young salesman who looked fresh out of high school greeted Barrett. "That one is a beauty. You looking for a boat?"

"I was just browsing. Thank you, though." Barrett smiled as he walked away, leaving the salesman with a frown.

When he got in his car, he tore open the envelope. He drew in a sharp breath as he immediately recognized the address in Crystal Beach. Uncle Elliott's estate.

Chapter 29

It had been several long days since Lottie last laid eyes on Barrett, and a gnawing sense of worry had settled within her. Where could he possibly be? Douglas remained frustratingly silent, leaving her to wonder if his absence was normal or something more troubling.

She curled up underneath her comforter and pulled out her Bible. She had twenty minutes before she needed to get ready for Bible class. She'd promised Samantha she'd be there and then join her family for a fajita luncheon. A smile crossed her face as she thought about her friendship with Samantha. It seemed real, not at all like Lottie expected.

Just as she began to delve into the comforting words of Matthew chapter 2, a sharp, insistent pecking interrupted her concentration. Who could that be? Since it was Sunday, she had the day off so surely it wasn't about work.

When Lottie opened the door, Alyssa burst into her room with an urgency that left little room for pleasantries. "I need an answer," she declared, her voice tinged with impatience.

Lottie furrowed her brow, confusion etched across her face. "An answer?"

"Do you need to make extra money or not?" Alyssa's eyes gleamed with determination.

"Of course, I need to make some money," Lottie replied cautiously, determined not to betray too much eagerness. She clutched the Bible to her chest like a shield. "But I'd like to know exactly what I'd be agreeing to first."

Alyssa took a step closer, her expression intense. "I need you to recruit young, attractive girls for my business."

"What business is that?" Lottie cocked her head as she retreated a few steps.

"I run an upscale escort service," Alyssa revealed. "We cater to the wealthiest clientele, and business is booming. I need a few more workers to keep up."

Lottie's eyes widened, and she shook her head. "You want me to find you some prostitutes?" she opened the door wider, a clear signal for Alyssa to leave. "I don't think so."

Alyssa stared at Lottie, shutting the door. "It's not like that," she insisted, her expression narrowing into a fierce glare. "Coco told me you were cool. Was he mistaken?"

Lottie froze, her heart racing at the mention of Coco's name. "You know Coco?"

A smirk played at the corner of Alyssa's lips. "Why do you think I approached you in the first place? I'm not an idiot."

"What kind of escort service do you run?"

"We're hired to enhance parties, to bring glamour to high-profile events, sometimes even as dates for the elite," Alyssa explained, her tone becoming more persuasive.

Lottie leaned against the doorframe, forcing her shoulders to relax. "Then why do you need me to recruit girls? Why not do it yourself?" She challenged, still pretending to be wary.

"Because I simply don't have the time," Alyssa replied, exasperation in her voice. "So, are you in or not?"

"Alright," she finally conceded. "I'm in."

"Very well. Make sure to bring me the first girl before the week is out," Alyssa instructed, her voice steady and commanding.

"A week? But I have work commitments." A shudder worked through Lottie's backbone.

"Yes, but Barrett won't mind letting you take time off if necessary. You don't need to fret about that," she replied dismissively, waving a hand as if to brush away her worries.

"He's my boss, but given that he's been absent for a while, maybe I could slip away unnoticed." Lottie's mind raced through the possibilities. She needed to speak to Barrett as soon as possible. She wasn't a good enough actress to pull something like this off. However, these girls needed her to help stop Alyssa's illegal activity. If she walked away, she'd never be able to live with herself. She swallowed the bile, threatening to come up. It could be Rhnae just as easily as anyone else.

A grin sprang across Alyssa's face. "Of course, he's been away. We've been in Orlando at my father's place."

A rush of heat flooded Lottie's face. "Oh... alright then."

"Don't forget. One girl by the end of the week." Alyssa crept forward, closing the space between them. She bound Lottie with a deadly stare. "And don't even think about saying anything to anyone about this. If you do, I'll bury you."

Two hours later, Lottie climbed into the pew behind Samantha and her kids. Samantha turned around and smiled.

Alvin Griffin, the preacher, started his sermon. "When you look in the mirror, what do you see? Many notice gray hairs, freckles, or wrinkles, while others struggle with feelings of ugliness or inadequacy. Some wear masks to conceal their inner battles, striving to meet expectations and fearing they fall short. We may remember our sins and worry that others see them, too, making it hard to recognize our true selves. But what matters most is not how we see ourselves, but how God sees us."

Lottie turned when someone slipped into the seat next to her. Barrett. She blinked a few times before meeting Samantha's shocked gaze. As Samantha turned around, tears glistened on her lashes.

"Please understand that God doesn't love us based on our appearance, intelligence, or accomplishments. He loves us simply because He is love. Nothing you do can change that love. It remains constant. When God looks at you, He doesn't see your flaws or what others see. He sees someone He loves and wishes to be closer to. So, when you look in the mirror, remember that you are treasured and beloved by God."

"Because you are a beloved child of God, trust Him and follow His way. Why? Because it works." He flipped through his Bible. "Turn with me to Matthew chapter 7, verses 7-11."

"Ask, and it will be given to you; seek, and you will find; knock, and it will be opened to you. For everyone who asks receives, and he who seeks finds, and to him who knocks, it will be opened. Or what man is there among you who, if his son asks for bread, will give him a stone? Or if he asks for a fish, will he give him a serpent? If you then, being evil, know how to give good gifts to your children, how much more will your Father who is in heaven give good things to those who ask Him!"

As Lottie listened to the preacher read the verses, she shifted in her seat. She glanced across the pew and locked eyes with Frosty. His sharp and inquisitive gaze sent an unexpected chill racing down her spine.

Chapter 30

After the closing prayer, Samantha wasted no time getting around the pew to hug Barrett. "I can't believe you're here."

He patted Samantha's back. "I can't either."

Brayden and Scarlett yelled hi to their uncle Barrett as they ran toward a group of kids playing around the pulpit.

Sylvia, the preacher's wife, greeted people as she walked down the aisle. She stopped beside Lottie and pulled her in for an embrace. "It's good to see you again, Lottie." She glanced at Barrett and stuck her hand out. "Hello again. It's good to see you here."

"Nice to see you again," Barrett said before turning around when Frosty called his name. "Excuse me."

A chill ran down Lottie's spine as she watched Barrett approach Frosty.

Sylvia glanced at Samantha. "Thanks for letting the kids come over this afternoon. My boys have been begging for a playdate."

"Oh, they're looking forward to it." As Samantha smiled, Lottie got the impression the kids weren't the only ones.

Sylvia continued down the aisle, and Samantha hoofed it to the pulpit when Brayden fell off the steps.

Lottie approached slowly, her footsteps soft against the carpet as she neared the spot where Frosty and Barrett stood engaged in conversation. A hint of a smile brushed her lips. "Hi."

"Hello there." Frosty returned her smile, twisting his body to face Lottie. "I just finished telling Barrett how much I enjoyed my stay at his bed and break-fast."

"Oh?" Lottie rested her hand on the nearest pew.

"Yes, it was my first time staying there, but it won't be my last."

A pang filled with hope struck her middle. "Are you leaving?"

"Yes, I'm on my way to my dealership in Tampa." He winked at Lottie. "It's been a pleasure seeing you again. I hope everything works out for you."

"You, too." Lottie found that her words were sin-cere.

"Let me know when you're ready for that job," he continued, his tone turning a bit more serious. "I have several dealerships across Florida. Take your pick."

After saying their goodbyes, Lottie rode with Samantha to her house for the promised lunch. The kids went with their friends for a playdate.

As the houses passed, Lottie found herself wondering if Frosty really had changed. He seemed different. And if she could change, why couldn't he?

About midway through the meal, Barrett glanced at Samantha. "Where did you say David is off to this time?"

Samantha shifted in her seat and took a sip of her root beer. "I told you he's at a convention in Salt Lake City for the weekend."

Barrett narrowed his eyes, suspicion written all over his face. "He's been to an awful lot of conventions lately."

"What are you getting at, Barrett?" Her tone laced with frustration.

He raised both hands. "Nothing, I'm just curious."

"He's just trying to build an empire, you know? He wants to make sure the kids have generational wealth that comes from him and not Mama's family."

"I get it. Sorry, didn't mean to touch a nerve."

"It's fine." Her tone softened. "What did you want to tell us?"

He recounted every detail of his meeting with Coco, the dinners with Alyssa and finally he shared that he'd stolen the contents from their uncle's safe.

As he spoke, Samantha's lashes flew high, and she let out a sharp gasp. "He'll never forgive you."

Barrett chewed a piece of ice from his lemonade, his mind seeming to work overtime. "I think he will once he understands we're trying to help."

Samantha pinched the bridge of her nose. "What was in the safe?"

After a brief pause, he spoke, frustration lacing his words. "A notebook and a contract."

"Well, don't keep us in suspense," Samantha urged, leaning forward on the table.

"The contract was between Uncle Elliott and James Blankenship. Uncle Elliott now owns Blankenship Oil."

"What?" Samantha leaned back into her chair. "How?"

"I don't know. What I do know is that Uncle Elliott is convinced James Blankenship had something to do with Chadwick's murder. It appears his goal in life is to ruin James."

Lottie sat up straighter in her chair. She recognized the name Chadwick from when she researched missing people from the rehab. "I'm sorry, I'm a bit out of the loop. Are you looking for drug dealers or a murderer?"

"Both," Barrett explained. He wiped a drop of lemonade from his chin with a purple napkin before continuing. "Our cousin was killed right at two years ago. We believe he got involved with the wrong crowd, but we're not sure what happened."

"So that's why you went undercover after leaving the Marines?" Lottie didn't bother trying to hide the curiosity etched across her face.

He wadded the napkin in his hand. "Yes."

"Makes sense." Lottie's mouth went dry as she considered the mess she'd gotten involved in. She would bow out. It wasn't her problem. But when she opened her mouth, she found she couldn't leave Samantha and Barrett high and dry. She had to help. "Alyssa asked me to work for her as a recruiter. She wants me to get young girls for her so-called family-friendly escort service."

"I knew she was bad news." Samantha slammed her fist on the table, causing Lottie's coffee cup to rattle.

Barrett laced his knuckles so tight they lost color. He traded a glance with Samantha. "Even though I didn't want to believe it, you were right about her."

"Did you find anything out while you were with Alyssa in Orlando?" Lottie asked, a hint of jealousy tinging her words.

"I don't know what you're talking about." Barrett's brow raised.

With a stubborn fold of her arms, Lottie met Barrett's curious gaze. "She told me you were with her at her father's place."

A spark of anger ignited in his eyes. "She's a liar. I've been busy working at Uncle Elliott's."

"Oh." Lottie swallowed the embarrassment as heat traveled up her neck.

Thankfully, Barrett decided not to give her a hard time, instead moving to a more important subject. "There's a female agent we can use as bait. In the meantime, I need to go to Orlando to dig deeper into how James Blankenship is tied to all this." Urgency laced Barrett's tone as he leaned forward. "It's vital we connect the dots before moving forward."

"Do we have an idea if the same people are working the home invasions, or is that another group?" Energy hummed through Lottie at the prospect of being involved in taking down the bad guys for once.

"I'm bringing in an agent I know from the CIA. We need help on this one." Barrett ran a hand through his hair, his eyes narrowing as he seemed to contemplate the situation. "Lottie, you just tell Alyssa you'll have someone soon. Act normal. I'll book the first flight out and we'll meet when I return."

Lottie nodded. "Be careful." She itched to reach across the table and take Barrett's hands in hers, but now was not the time. Maybe after all this was over, she'd get the chance.

Chapter 31

After telling Alyssa she'd have someone soon, Lottie had dodged her for the past two days. She pulled her hair into a messy bun before brushing her teeth. Counseling had mentally drained her today, so she looked forward to curling up with her Bible and a heating pad.

Barrett hadn't made it back from Orlando. Hopefully he would find something incriminating and come home soon. Lottie still couldn't believe wealthy, upstanding people like the Blankenship's would be involved in criminal activity. On the other hand, anyone with a love for money and power could be easily led to do things they wouldn't otherwise.

As she pulled out her nightgown, the phone on her nightstand rang. Her brow furrowed, but she picked it up. "Hello?"

"Lottie, it's Mildred. I hate to ask, but our overnight desk attendant called in sick. Douglas is not feeling well. Is there any way I can get you to take the shift?"

Lottie cast a longing look at the comfy bed and Bible beside her pillow. "I can do that."

"You have no idea how much I appreciate you. How soon can you be down here?"

"Give me ten minutes." Lottie would've said no, but Douglas was an older man, and Mildred wasn't up to an overnight shift.

"Thank you, Lottie. See you soon." She said before the line disconnected.

An hour later, Lottie stood beside the bay window, gazing into the night. The deep indigo canvas, sprinkled with twinkling stars shimmering like scattered diamonds, took her breath away. In the distance, a hauntingly beautiful sliver of a muted orange moon hung low, its soft glow illuminating the landscape with an ethereal light. She'd never seen a dark circular outline framing the entire moon like this night.

"Lottie."

As soon as Lottie heard her name, she whorled about. Alyssa stood there, wearing black leggings and an oversized black short-sleeved sweatshirt. She looked like the perfect athlete, with her long hair tucked into a ponytail and a black ballcap on her head.

"Good evening, Alyssa."

An artificial smile graced her lips. "I need to grab something from my room, but when I get back, we need to talk."

"About?" Lottie asked, drifting around the counter.

"You haven't lived up to your end of the bargain."

"I told you I have someone and will set it up."

Alyssa narrowed her eyes before walking up the stairs.

With tingling fingers, Lottie reached for her phone. Only to come up empty-handed. She closed her eyes and let out a deep breath. She had plugged it into the charger before Mildred called. She must've left it in her room.

No big deal. She would act normal, like Barrett said.

Forty-five minutes later Lottie glanced at her watch. Where could Alyssa be? Hopefully asleep. Lottie couldn't get that lucky.

With a grumbling stomach, Lottie opened a Milky Way and grabbed a bottle of root beer. She loved the taste of crisp root beer from a glass bottle.

Rhnae bustled through the front door and stopped inside. Her hopeful gaze drove all the breathable air from Lottie's body and threw normal out the window. Rhnae had no business being here right now.

"I got your text." She took a few tentative steps toward Lottie and dropped her backpack on the floor.

"What text?" Lottie asked, her heart gunning into overdrive as she gaped at Rhnae.

"Also, Frankie told me what you've been up to."

"She told you what? And what text?"

"She said you're trying to do something good, and I would be so proud of you," Rhnae said, her eyes brimming with tears as she stepped behind the counter, pointing her phone screen at Lottie.

> I need to see you. Can you come to the address I'm about to share?

> Tonight?

> Yes, quickly. It's very important.

> Okay. OMW

Lottie gasped, her stomach sinking with dread. She gathered Rhnae into her arms and kissed her forehead. "I promise to tell you all about it. But right now, I need you to get to your car as quickly as possible and drive home."

"Why?" Rhnae backed out of Lottie's embrace. "Don't you want to see me? Why did you ask me to come then?"

"Of course I want to see you, but I'm working on something I don't want you in the middle of." Lottie cupped Rhnae's face and looked deep into her eyes, imploring her to listen.

"Okay. I'll leave, but are you safe?" Rhnae's eyes tightened at the corners. "You're acting weird."

"I'm fine. Please listen to me." Lottie held her breath as she waited for Rhnae to leave.

With a nod, Rhnae picked up her backpack and smiled. "I love you, and I'm sorry for what I said."

"Oh, baby, I'm sorry too, and I promise I'll do everything I can to be the mother you deserve."

"Well, well. You promised a girl, and I will say that I'm not disappointed." Alyssa's voice caused a prickle of fear to rampage Lottie's body. "Hello, Rhnae."

Lottie drilled her gaze into Rhnae's. "Run."

Rhnae shook her head. "I'm not leaving you."

"Now." As a memory of the last day they spent with Eddie overwhelmed Lottie's senses, the urgency in her tone left no room for argument. She would not allow her child to be assaulted. Or worse.

Rhnae's eyes doubled in size, and she nodded before her legs jolted into motion toward the door.

Coco appeared from out of nowhere, blocking Rhnae inside. He lowered his gaze. "I'm sorry, Lottie."

A sharp pain sliced through Lottie's skull, causing the strength to leave her legs. As her body crashed onto the floor, she opened her eyes a slit. Only to find an empty room.

THEN: 2022

How would Lottie get past losing her only sister and then her best friend? It had been years, but the wounds hadn't healed. How much drugs and alcohol would it take? She didn't know but had every intention of finding out.

After washing a pill down with the last swig of whiskey from her current bottle, she pitched it across the room. It bounced into the wall with a bang, shattering onto the dirty tile kitchen floor.

The man sitting across the table from Lottie looked bug-eyed at her. His greasy brown hair hung in his face, and he reminded Lottie of a possum with a mullet. "What's your problem?"

She blinked a few times, trying to recall his name. Carl? No. Brad? Maybe, but probably not. "Don't worry about it," Lottie slurred. "This is my house, and I can break things if I want to."

He laced a joint with a powdery substance before lighting it and taking a deep drag. "Two can play that game."

"What do you mean by that?" Lottie unscrewed the top off another whiskey bottle and popped another pill.

He handed her the joint with a crooked smile. "You'll see."

She inhaled a few puffs before handing it back when the room started spinning. "I'm about done."

After another drag, he laid the joint in the ashtray and stood. He doubled up his fist and hit Lottie on the side of her head. The chair teetered into the wall. Fiery slices of pain shot through her leg as it bent backward when she whacked the hard tile.

"Get out!" Rhnae screamed at the man as she pointed a handgun at his chest.

Where would her thirteen-year-old daughter get a gun? Fear replaced the pain as she watched the scene unfold.

He picked up the dope and slipped it in his pocket before raising his hands. "I'm leaving, you little snot," he exclaimed on his way out the door.

Rhnae locked the door behind him and hoofed it over to Lottie. "Mama! What happened?"

Lottie's eyes drifted closed. She wanted to explain to Rhnae that this would be the last time, but her voice wouldn't work.

It seemed like minutes, yet weeks, since Lottie had seen Rhnae. A steady beeping sound caused her to stir. She cracked her eyes open and met a blast from the past. "Robin?"

Her old friend from Miami grasped Lottie's hand. Her once long dark hair had been cut to a short bob. "Hi, Lottie. I got a call when you were admitted. I'm still listed as your emergency contact."

"Oh. Thank you for coming all this way." Lottie pressed her fingers into her forehead. "Have you seen Rhnae?"

Robin narrowed her eyes. "Not only did you have a man Rhnae didn't recognize in your apartment, but he also broke your arm, she pulled a gun on him, and you managed to overdose all in one day."

Lottie swallowed and darted her eyes to the whiteboard hanging on the wall. Her vision zeroed in on Jennifer, her nurse's name. "I messed up."

"You messed up? I'd say so," Robin scolded. "When you left Miami, I just knew you'd turn your life around. Never did I expect you to be in this mess."

"It wasn't intentional."

"It never is." Robin's tone softened. "Lottie, the state took custody of Rhnae."

"What?" Lottie's heart raced as a deathly sick feeling curdled her stomach.

"You need to get your life on track and put your daughter first for once. It's now or never."

Those words echoed in Lottie's mind as she struggled to keep her eyes open. "I will. I promise I will change."

Going six months without drugs had not been easy. The judge was unreasonable, Lottie thought as she guzzled a swig of whiskey. He wanted her off everything, including alcohol, before he'd consider putting Rhnae back in her custody.

What was his problem? Whiskey was legal. As she took another swig, she realized she'd lost count of how many bottles she'd had.

She left her tiny apartment and headed down the side road, a bottle of whiskey under her arm. Maybe a walk in the cool night air would clear her head.

Within a few minutes of leaving, she stumbled down an alley behind a row of stores. She slid down the wall and pondered her life as she finished the bottle.

She couldn't tell how long she'd been in that alley when meows from a cat woke her. A muscle ticked under her eye as she thrust her gaze upward. The morning sun rose on the horizon, leaving a pinkish hue across the sky.

As she sat up, she grabbed her head. Dried vomit covered her cheek and neck, and her clothes reeked like a month-old garbage bag. A white and gray spotted cat sat a few feet away, its gaze clamped onto Lottie almost as if it pitied her situation.

She stared back at the cat, unable to look away as it anchored its golden gaze to hers. A lump of air caught in her chest as she considered what that cat saw when it looked at her. Finally, she unlocked her gaze from the cat's and turned away, her collarbone hot with shame.

Unsure why it took a cat's pitiful gaze to make her take stock of her life, she stood on wobbly legs. "I will do better, " she said, partially to the cat, mostly to herself. "From this moment on, I will not touch another drug or drink alcohol. I promise."

As Lottie slogged down the alley, she looked back at the cat with a half-smile. "Thank you."

Chapter 33

Present Day

The trip to Orlando had been a bust. If James Blankenship had anything to do with Chadwick's death, he had buried anything that could tie him to it.

After taking a late-night flight from Orlando to Destin, Barrett's weary bones ached, and he couldn't wait to soak in a tub. He clicked his blinker to turn into the bed and breakfast, and he frowned. Something seemed off.

Maybe the eerie moon and dark sky had him feeling a bit uneasy. It looked stunning, but if he believed in zombies, he'd expect a trove of them to come out from behind the building.

As he opened the front door, he chuckled at his silliness. All signs of laughter vanished as he laid eyes on Lottie lying on the ground with Douglas and Mildred whispering beside her.

Mildred wheeled her chair around. "Oh, Barrett we are so thankful to see you. Douglas was just about to call an ambulance."

He dropped his overnight bag and thundered toward them, his heart pounding so hard it vibrated his throat. "What happened?"

"We think she hit her head," Douglas replied as he helped Lottie to her feet. "I was already in bed when I heard a commotion in here. By the time I got up and dressed, Mildred said poor Lottie here had passed out."

Barrett scooped Lottie into his arms and took off toward the door. "I'm getting you to the hospital."

"Why don't you let Douglas call an ambulance?" Mildred raised her voice as Barrett held the door open with his foot.

"No, this will be faster."

"Wait a minute." Mildred's voice turned urgent. "You need to know what happened."

Barrett ignored her pleas and kept going until he tucked Lottie into the front seat of his Camaro. He hopped inside, put the car in reverse, and gunned the engine.

Within a few minutes, Lottie stirred. "Barrett?"

"I'm here." He gripped her hand with his. "I'm getting you to the hospital."

"No!" A cry spilled out of Lottie as despair flowed from her eyes. "I'll be fine."

"Why not? What happened?"

"They took Rhnae."

His stomach churned. "What? Who?"

"Alyssa and Coco." She wiped her tears. "We have to find her. I don't care what it takes."

His grip on Lottie's hand intensified. "We will find her."

She rubbed the back of her head with her free hand and winced. "I think Douglas hit me from behind."

His nostrils flared. "Douglas? Are you sure?"

"It wasn't Alyssa and Coco was by the door when I got hit. Who else could it be?"

He let go of Lottie's hand and picked up his phone. After talking to someone about the bed and breakfast, he took Lottie's hand in his again. He pulled into the empty parking lot of Silver Sands Outlet and met her misty gaze. "I'm so sorry I dragged you into this."

"This isn't your fault. Just find her."

"I put a tracker in Alyssa's purse when we had dinner," Barret said as he pulled out a tablet and tapped on the screen. "Got her."

"Where is she?"

He coked his head. "At the docks. On my boat."

By the time they made it across Destin to the docks, the night seemed darker than ever. They made their way toward Barrett's boat as quietly as possible. On the very top deck lay the tracking device with a note.

If you want your daughter, give me Barrett.

Chapter 34

Never in her life would Lottie have dreamed she'd be standing on a dock with the man of her dreams, listening to him agree to swap his life for her daughter's.

"I understand," he spoke into the phone. "No cops. Lottie and I will be waiting for you. Just us."

After ending the call, he sent a few messages. "I'm letting Samantha know what's happened." He turned to Lottie, bringing her hand to his heart. "I asked Samantha to pray for us—especially you and Rhnae. Whatever happens, promise me you'll find happiness."

"Barrett…"

"It's my fault you're in this situation. I should've pushed you into your Jeep and out of the parking lot that first night we met."

"Why didn't you?"

"Even then, I was drawn to you. I just didn't realize how much."

She sobbed. "I feel the same way."

He touched her chin, lifting her face to meet his. "Hey. It's going to be all right. I've been dreaming of our first kiss for a while now, so it has to be."

Her stomach somersaulted as she drew in a sharp breath. "Tomorrow?"

"Yes, tomorrow." Lights from an incoming boat shined in their eyes. Barrett took a step back as a firm resolve entered his gaze. "Let's get your daughter."

With a glare at Barrett, Big Levi helped Alyssa out of the boat. Before Lottie or Barrett could move, Alyssa pulled out a handgun. She affixed Barrett with an unblinking gaze. "You shouldn't have lied to me about your relationship with that woman."

"Alyssa, this is not you. Let's take a step back and figure things out."

"You should've realized Mildred would tell me everything." Her lower lip quivered. "We could've gotten back together. Instead you chose a drug addict."

Lottie took a step forward. "Where is my daughter? You promised you'd bring her."

"I suppose Barrett isn't the only liar. You should've stayed away from him. I told you we were getting back together," she said as she stomped her foot on the dock.

"How did you know about Rhnae?"

"I saw her picture on your phone and did some checking. It wasn't hard."

"Alyssa, please take me and leave Rhnae with her mother." Barrett took a step toward Alyssa.

"This is for lying to me." As she pulled the trigger, the bullet whizzed past Lottie, close enough that she nearly felt it in the air. It hit Barrett in the chest. He fell to the ground in slow motion. Lottie shrieked, reaching for Barrett.

Big Levi grabbed her in a bear hug and carried her to the waiting boat. She landed with a thud on the floor as Alyssa's laughter echoed across the water.

"Where's Rhnae?" Lottie ignored the throbbing in her skull as she found her footing.

Alyssa folded her lips together. "You know it really is a shame."

"Take me to my daughter."

"I had high hopes that you would be able to replace Mildred, but like Barrett, you disappointed me."

"What do you mean?" Lottie jerked against the handcuffs, cutting into her wrists. They didn't budge. "Where's my child?"

"Mildred is getting too old for this line of work. You were to be the perfect replacement. But now, you and your daughter will both be sold."

"Sold?"

"You both know too much." She nodded at Big Levi. He disappeared through a door. When he returned, Coco followed behind with Rhnae in his grasp. Coco lowered his gaze to the floor, shame evident on his face.

Lottie's heart rate skyrocketed. "Baby girl, are you okay?"

Rhnae nodded, fear evident in her gaze.

Lottie wished she could tell Rhnae about the hidden device in her sandal, but there was no way she could risk Alyssa finding out. That tiny tracker was her only hope that she and Rhnae would make it out of this alive. Lottie had no doubt that Barrett would come for her and Rhnae.

The boat skimmed over the water, picking up speed as it hit wave after wave, causing Lottie's head to throb a little more. She closed her eyes and prayed for the strength to make it through.

Alyssa's voice interrupted Lottie's prayer. "I hope you don't think Barrett will be coming for you."

Lottie glared at Alyssa but stayed quiet.

"He's a crook, you know. Mildred told me how you and Barrett have been sneaking around. But what you don't know is he has been using you."

"I don't believe you."

"Yeah, he set you up." She tapped a button on her phone. "Listen for yourself."

Barrett's voice filled the area.

"There's no way your daddy will let you get back together with... a person like me."

"You let me deal with Daddy. Tell me, are you involved with the lady working for you?"

"Who?"

"What's her name...Lucy? No, her name is Lottie."

"Oh, her? Samantha hired her without even asking me. I think she's there to make a little money and then leave."

"What makes you say that?"

"I've seen a lot of people like her over the years. The type who work a job for a few weeks only to get money to support their habit, then they disappear."

"So you think she's just there for a paycheck?"

"Until you asked, I haven't given it much thought. She's doing a necessary job. After that, what she does is none of my business."

"What would you say if I could get you a job where you'd never have to answer to your uncle again?"

"I'd say that's too good to be true."

Alyssa slid the phone into her pocket and grinned wickedly at Lottie. "See what I mean? Barrett doesn't care about you."

Lottie lowered her head as a teardrop fell. She'd gone most of her life feeling less than. And there was no way she'd allow this woman to continue the trend. Lottie squared her shoulders and met Alyssa's gaze. "You're a liar. I know Barrett. He's not with you."

Alyssa drew in a breath. "Mildred found your phone. You were very foolish to leave it on your nightstand."

"What do you mean?"

Alyssa laughed as she turned to Rhnae. "Sorry to tell you, but that text asking you to meet your mama was from me, you know."

Rhnae's eyes widened as she stared at Lottie. Lottie met Rhnae's gaze. "Don't worry, Barrett will get us out of here. I promise."

The boat drifted to a stop. Large waves hit the side of the boat, tilting them to the right and then left. Alyssa sat at the booth and answered her phone, speaking in a muffled tone.

Once she hung up, she grabbed Lottie's face and stared into her eyes. "Your ride to your new homes will be here shortly. Looks like Barrett didn't make it in time to save you after all."

Lottie glared at Alyssa, her mind working to devise a plan in case Barrett was hurt worse than she thought.

Alyssa walked away, stopping in front of Rhnae. She picked up a lock of her dark hair and smiled. "Levi, take this one into the other room and chain her up."

Even though Lottie's hands were cuffed, she bolted toward Alyssa. Their bodies smacked, and they both tumbled onto the floor. Levi pulled Lottie off Alyssa with her hair.

Rhnae screamed something that wasn't legible as Levi slung Lottie into the window. Her already pounding head throbbed when it hit the glass, cracking it slightly.

As Levi came at Rhnae a second time, Coco jumped in between them. He flicked his knife and jotted it toward Levi. "Stay back, man."

Alyssa let out a whiny groan. "What is it with men wanting to rescue this woman?"

Coco ignored Alyssa. "Lottie, forgive me for my part in this. I had no idea it was your daughter Alyssa wanted me to grab when she asked me to come to the bed and breakfast."

Levi pulled a knife from his waistband and threw it at Coco, burying it in his shoulder. Coco's body jerked. He shot a regretful gaze at Lottie as his knife clunked at his feet. "I'm sorry."

"Throw him overboard," Alyssa demanded.

Levi grabbed Coco and headed out the only door. Within seconds, a big splash sounded in the night, mingling with Lottie's sobs.

Chapter 35

The breath flew out of Barrett before his back hit the hard dock. Even though the bullet lodged in his vest, a sharp pain tore through his chest.

Cody Davenport's boots vibrated the docks as he barreled toward Barrett. "Are you hit?"

"My vest stopped it." Barrett choked out.

Cody, a CIA Agent Barrett had met a few years back, helped Barrett to his feet. "I have a few boats with teams ready to go."

"Let's go," Barrett said as he pulled up the tracker app. "I have their location."

A text message from Coco appeared on the screen.

Pick up the phone and mute it

Within seconds, his phone rang. He followed instructions and muted his audio before placing it on speaker.

Alyssa's voice flowed through the speaker. *"Your ride to your new homes will be here shortly. Looks like Barrett didn't make it in time to save you after all."*

Barrett met Cody's curios gaze. "We need to hurry." He said as he stepped onto the boat.

"Levi, take this one into the other room and chain her up."

Someone tussled in the background. A girl screamed.

"Stay back, man."

That sounded like Coco. Within seconds, Coco spoke again. *"I'm sorry."*

The next words sent a chill to Barrett's core. *"Throw him overboard."*

Cody glanced at Barrett, the same apprehension in his gaze that Barrett felt in his bones. "Did she say throw him or her overboard?"

"I couldn't tell. It was too muted."

Barrett unmuted his audio. "Alyssa, I promise I'm coming for you. Don't do anything that will get you in deeper. Let Lottie and Rhnae go."

Just as Barrett thought things couldn't get worse, a big splash sounded in the night, and the call ended. He had no idea if she'd heard what he said, but he intended to keep that promise.

With Coco's dropped knife in her hand, Lottie positioned her body in front of Rhnae. The handcuffs would make it hard to stab someone, but she'd figure it out. Even with beads of sweat rolling down her cheeks, her lips drew into a hard line. She'd die before Levi or Alyssa touched her child. "Stay back."

Alyssa's lips edged up at the corners, and she giggled as she eyeballed Levi. "Just let her stay there with her little knife. Their ride is almost here."

The whirring of an approaching boat caused Lottie's stomach to churn. If Barrett didn't show up, she'd have to be ready to protect Rhnae.

Two men stalked inside the cabin a few minutes after the other boat arrived. The older of the two smiled at Lottie, showing perfectly straight white teeth. "Alyssa, my peach, you've done well. I may keep this one for myself."

Several men decked out in all black, carrying guns, flooded the room. Barrett pointed a gun at the man's head. "Over my dead body, James."

A flood of emotion warmed Lottie's insides. "Barrett," she said, breaking into a smile.

Tears poured down Alyssa's face as she stared at the man who had suggested keeping Lottie. "How could you let this happen, Daddy?"

Daddy?

Rhnae wrapped her hands around Lottie. "I take it this is the Barrett you said would come for us?"

Lottie nodded. "It is, baby girl."

The agents handcuffed the criminals and led them away with Alyssa screeching the entire time.

Barrett moved across the cabin. "Are you both okay?" he asked as he unlocked Lottie's handcuffs.

"Amazingly, but they threw Coco overboard." Lottie flinched as she rubbed her wrists.

"We found him barely treading water," Barrett said, his gaze locked on Lottie's face. "He's on one of our boats getting sewed up."

Lottie stared at the bruises forming on her wrists. "That's such a relief."

Barrett glanced at Rhnae. "I'm Barrett. You must be the daughter Lottie always talks about."

Rhnae wrapped her arms tightly around Barrett, her eyes shimmering with unshed tears that reflected the deep relief coursing through her. "Thank you for saving us," she whispered, her voice quivering with emotion.

"You're welcome," Barrett replied gently, returning her embrace with a warmth that melted Lottie's heart. After a brief moment, he hesitated, then asked, "Would it be okay if I kiss your mother?"

A bright grin spread across Rhnae's face, a hint of mischief dancing in her eyes as she released him. "Go for it," she encouraged.

As Barrett turned his attention to Lottie, her heart raced, and her thoughts swirled in a dizzying blend of surprise and gratitude. He leaned closer, brushing a few strands of hair away from her face with a tenderness that made her breath catch. "I'm so glad you and Rhnae aren't hurt," he murmured, locking his gaze onto hers with an intensity that turned her knees to mush.

With a delicate touch, he lifted her hand and pressed a soft, lingering kiss to her knuckles. The knees that had turned to mush now threatened to cave in.

As Lottie met Rhnae's approving gaze, her heart sang with joy. Even though they had a long road to get where they needed to be as a family, she had no doubt God would continue to watch over and guide them along the way.

Chapter 36

As the morning dawn broke across the sky, Barrett eased into a parking spot at the bed and breakfast. Across the street, a motorcycle rumbled to life. The driver glanced at them before speeding down the street.

Rhnae lay in the back seat, a bunched-up blanket under her neck. Lottie's eyes shone with love as she watched her daughter sleep. "I hope that's the last adventure she has at sea."

"Me, too," Barrett replied.

Samantha and another woman bustled down the steps and stopped in front of Lottie. The three embraced, tears flowing freely.

"I called you so many times, Aunt Lottie," the woman said as she stepped back. "I had to know if Rhnae was safe."

"My phone has been in my room all night. I'm sorry."

"No, it's not your fault. I didn't realize Rhnae left until almost ten."

A tall man with the reddest hair Barrett had ever seen came from the bed and breakfast. He hugged Lottie before looking inside the car at Rhnae. "We thought she was in her room." He turned to Barrett and stuck his hand out. "I'm Alex Foster. I understand we owe you a great deal of thanks."

"No thanks necessary," Barrett said as he shook Alex's hand.

Rhnae stepped out of the back seat. "I'm sorry. I shouldn't have left like that, but I wanted to see that Mama was doing okay."

Samantha leaned into Barrett for a second before her bossiness kicked in. "Let's get inside. Frankie and I made breakfast."

After breakfast, Samantha pulled Barrett aside. "I still can't believe Mildred has been in on the home invasions and everything else this whole time. Have you heard anything about Douglas?"

"Nothing other than his heart attack. I plan to visit him today."

"You don't think he was in on it?"

"From what Cody says, there's no evidence to show Douglas had a part in any of it," Barrett spoke to Samantha, but he couldn't take his eyes off Lottie as she walked down the stairs.

Wet hair clung to her shoulders, and she'd changed into a baby blue sweatsuit. It looked like she covered her bruises. His breath strangled in his throat, and he found that no words would come out.

Samantha lightly shoved him on the shoulder. "Go talk to her."

He nodded, striding toward the woman who owned his heart.

Lottie had no intention of untangling her gaze from Barrett's as she came down the staircase. She held her hand out when they met at the bottom of the stairs.

He took her hand and led her out the back door toward the gazebo. They sat down, his hand firmly attached to hers. "How's Rhnae?"

"She and Frankie are both sound asleep in my bed." She smiled. "I believe Alex is having a second helping of breakfast."

"I've spent the better part of the past ten years clinging to a solitary existence. Even when I was engaged, I never felt like I had someone by my side. I had no room for God in my life. But without God, I don't believe we would be here."

"I agree. Prayers have gotten me through years full of trials and heartaches, Barrett." She paused, her gaze drifting to their entwined hands before slowly lifting her gaze to his. "You are an answer to one of my most fervent prayers, a blessing I never saw coming."

He leaned his forehead to hers, his voice coming out a mere whisper. "I believe He put us together for a reason."

"From the moment I met Samantha, I sensed a shift in my life. Who knew the choices I made that night would lead me to you?"

"You saved my nephew and played a pivotal role in bringing criminals to justice, all the while capturing my heart along the way."

"For a long time, I believed my life was for nothing."

"You were wrong. You are my world, Lottie McKenna. I need you to remember that, no matter what challenges lie ahead." Barrett choked back a sob. "I want to be a better man for you. I've been reading the Bible, and I agreed to start studying with the preacher. Will you come to church with me Sunday?"

"Yes! Of course, I will come." She raised her face to his, her laughter mingling with tears of joy.

With a tender glimmer in his eyes, he leaned in closer and softly asked, "May I kiss you?"

That familiar heat she'd grown to embrace since meeting Barrett warmed her cheeks. "I may strangle you if you don't," she replied right before entwining her lips with his.

Epilogue

F airy lights twinkled softly around the gazebo, casting a warm, enchanting glow over the festivities. Tall palm trees stood around the area, their leaves rustling gently in the evening breeze and enhancing the tropical atmosphere. An elegantly set grand table large enough for twelve sat in the middle of the gazebo.

Despite the laughter and chatter of the people around her, Lottie's gaze remained captivated by Barrett. He stood with an air of confidence, his deep blue sweater fitting snugly around his arms.

With a glint in his eye, he raised a glass of sparkling water high above his head. "Let's raise our glasses to the birthday girl." He smiled when Rhnae handed Lottie a small white box with a gold ribbon on the top. Anticipation filled her gaze as she glanced from the gift to Barrett, who continued, "Happy Birthday, Lottie. I can never thank God enough for seeing fit to put you in my life. I love you."

Lottie embraced the magical moment. She'd never had anyone do something like this for her, and his words filled her heart with joy.

Rhnae leaned close to Lottie's ear. "It's diamond earrings. Don't worry, though. He's saving the engagement ring for our Christmas party."

Lottie's eyes sparkled as she absorbed Rhnae's words. She carefully opened the delicate velvet box. Inside lay a stunning set of heart-shaped diamond earrings shimmering brilliantly in the soft light. Her breath hitched as she met Barrett's gaze, so full of warmth and adoration. "Thank you, Barrett," she finally managed to say, her voice overwhelmed with the emotion of the moment. "I love you so much."

Her heart swelled as she cast her eyes around the table full of family and friends. Even Barrett's Uncle Elliott had made an appearance. He was guarded, but she knew he'd faced many heartaches. His son, Chadwick, had started taking drugs after a boating accident left him injured. From there, he fell in with the wrong crowd and ended up getting killed by Levi. Elliott had purchased James Blankenship's business, with every intention of ruining James and his family. James planned to steal it back but had been thwarted by Barrett.

They had no idea why Levi killed Chadwick, but Coco had testified against him and the others in court. For that, Coco was put in protective custody, and Lottie would probably never see him again. He started working with Alyssa after they met in Alabama. He had no problem selling drugs or robbing people but drew the line when it came to hurting Lottie and Rhnae. She prayed he would be able to live a life with purpose. Ultimately, he had tried to protect her and Rhnae, so there was some good in him.

Alyssa gave her father up as the leader and received a shorter sentence but would still be in prison for a long time. Mildred hit Lottie with her root beer bottle when they took Rhnae. Turned out, her back had healed but she pretended to be hurt just to spy on Barrett and Lottie. Poor Douglas had been shocked that his wife could be so cruel. After recovering from the heart attack, he begged for their forgiveness before he moved to Mississippi. Lottie prayed he would eventually be able to deal with the betrayal and hurt and move on with his life.

Amazingly, Frosty really was a changed man. He had no dealings with the criminals and was saddened to lose Coco as an employee and friend. He still wanted Lottie to work for him, but she'd chosen to decline his offer. Instead, she'd be working at Next Chapter Rehab as a counselor as soon as she became certified. She couldn't wait! Especially for Rhnae, who would move in with Lottie after graduating in a few months.

Frankie's husband, Alex, smiled at Lottie from across the table. She smiled back, remembering their first meeting when she was near rock bottom. He had invited her to church, and she reminded him she was a recovering drug addict. His response had been, "I heard you say you're a recovering drug addict. Either way, you're welcome in the Lord's church."

Alex helped her by offering a few encouraging words when she needed them. Now, her goal in life was to do the same for someone else.

She had Barrett, a slew of people encouraging her, and God guiding her. That was more than enough.

Thank you for taking the time to read **Lottie's Journey.** If you found it enjoyable, I would be grateful if you would leave a review. Your feedback truly makes a difference!

acknowledgments

I want to start by expressing my gratitude to my readers. Your willingness to embrace this genre-hopping, all-over-the-place writer gives me hope and inspires me to keep writing!

My beautiful cover model, Tammy Gaddy, and I have been friends for a long time, and I'm incredibly grateful she agreed to be on the cover of this deeply personal book. Love you!

A huge thank you goes to my wonderful beta reader, Vickie Mink, for taking the time to read my work and providing invaluable advice that improved the flow of the manuscript. I also want to extend my heartfelt appreciation to my sister-in-law, Brandie Hudson, for her incredible talent in reading and offering such great suggestions.

I also want to express my heartfelt gratitude to Robert Stephens and Regina Hagen for diving deep into this novel and giving me fantastic feedback and suggestions. I owe a huge thanks to Regina's mom, Francis, whose amazing proofreading skills really helped polish the final manuscript.

I couldn't have done this without my husband, Mark, and my sweet daughters, Cassidy and Carissa. Thank you for putting up with my endless chatter about my characters and stories and for joining me on our fun research trips – I know hitting the beach is a tough job, right? Haha! Cassidy, your insights into the final version were invaluable. I love you all so much!

Many people contributed to bringing this novel together, and I can't thank you all enough!

Much love,

Leah

about the author

Author Leah Brewer enjoys a fulfilling life in a small town in Arkansas with her husband of nearly nineteen years and their family. She cannot function until she's had her morning coffee (or maybe that should say won't). Leah loves writing HEA stories, with the goal of helping people smile, grow closer to God, and find their happy place.

Feel free to connect with Leah on Facebook at facebook.com/writingleahbrewer or check out her work on her website at www.theleahjournal.com.

www.ingramcontent.com/pod-product-compliance
Lightning Source LLC
Chambersburg PA
CBHW020112310726
48970CB00002B/594